Maciej Wojtkiewicz

JULIA vs OLYMPICS

A Novellette

AP PRESS
First Edition
1 3 5 7 9 10 8 6 4 2
This book is set in 12-point Calluna.
ISBN 978-83-950497-0-5 (paperback)
ISBN 978-83-950497-1-2 (e-book)
Visit www.azanpictures.com

To Julia

TABLE OF CONTENTS

CHAPTER ONE: HOME............................. 1
CHAPTER TWO: THE HEADPIECE 37
CHAPTER THREE: THE MIRROR 107
ACKNOWLEDGMENTS 151
EXTRAS: SYNCHRO GLOSSARY 153
EXTRAS: MAKING OF 161

JULIA vs OLYMPICS

CHAPTER ONE
Home

IT WAS THAT RARE MOMENT when the golden, yellowish-brown stream of light was reflecting inside the irises of Julie's eyes, making them more bright and coruscating than the green diamonds or the stars in the dusts of Pillars of Creation. But she didn't know that.

She was standing on the deck, before the start, ready for her final solo routine. Late afternoon. Dim, yet honey-warm light was sketching her silhouette, her arms raised for the crowd, her swimsuit gleaming with thousands of sequins, her legs crossed in a pose for the life-changing feat.

She was courageous, she was proud, she was—in

three minutes—winning the Olympics.

First step. Chin up and to the left, and then the smile for the constellation thousand light years above.

She saw the floor, few tiles beneath her feet, the scene, lots of dark, brownish dots, a small wall before the edge of the pool. A step up and then her hands straight ahead and crossed.

She was in the air, upside down, touching with her fingers the firm surface of the water. Less than a second, and she will be in. And suddenly, she stopped in her flight, in the same way as something stopped inside her body. She was frozen in a feeling of fear in her chest and belly, strong enough to hold her against the gravity in her fall.

She forgot about the music.

"Enough daydreaming, Julie!" the coach was now really angry. "Don't you sleep in the night?"

"I don't have the time to sleep. I'm too busy!" she answered instantly. "But don't think," Julie looked at Vikki and Ivy, who had just arrived to the edge of the pool, "I'm only doing the cooking during my bedtime."

"Dive!"

The meaning of the command was simple—

crawl, two laps while holding breath, best time won.

First few meters were always very nice. The lack of the need for breathing was making every single stroke easier and faster. And then—it was usually in the middle of the pool, after seven or eight cycles—came this uneasy feeling of tickling in the neck.

She was wearing dark leggings and a white shirt on her Funkita, just to create more drag in the water. She didn't feel it well, only the wetness of her sleeves.

The floor underneath changed a little. Tiles had become more bright and full of flickering, tiny streams of light. The turn was in a few seconds. A nice flip, she felt the air and then the wall with her feet. For a moment Julie thought about breathing. Her neck was quite itchy.

It was the time to speed up, less than a half of the pool to the end. The muscles in her neck contracted a few times, and she forced her head down once or twice as the bluish light on the right side of the pool marked the last three meters of her swim.

First four breaths were short and shallow, Julie caught the steel bar below the starting platform and leaned against the cold wall of the pool. She had on her face two tiny streams of water, going down alongside with a few strands of her hair sticking out from under her swimming cup.

"Heart rate check, counting!"

Julie raised her back from the side of the pool and touched her neck just above the collarbone. "Twenty-nine," she answered for the next call from the coach after ten seconds.

"Not too bad," she said to Julie with a slight satisfaction. "Ivy, the heart rate, counting!"

Ivy finished the dive just a few seconds ago and now she was standing next to Julie, open-mouthed, with small droplets of water on her chest, counting the beats of her hearth, moved by a little thrill with each one of them. She was looking at the coach while trying to correlate her breaths, pulse and counting. Her skin, hair, swimming cup—all they were gray or dark-blue in the dim, artificial lighting of their swimming hall.

"Twenty-eight!" Ivy shouted with a quite brisk voice.

"That's even better," said the coach. "Eggbeater with hands, to your count."

"But, Mia, we are too tired!" Julie said.

"The training is for you to be tired. You will rest at home."

"I don't—"

"Julie, you have the lead!"

They swam—or maybe walked without touching the ground—in a row. She was the first one, Ivy right behind her, then Vikki and Kenzie with Chloe at the end. The water—watched from above the surface—was greeny with a slight aquamarine cast. On the deck their coaches, Mia and others, were going slowly, with the speed of their swim.

Julie was the counter, so except swimming she had to set the rhythm for the whole pool by very loud shouting.

"One, two, three, four, five!"

Every "five" they had one vertical jump or "boost," ideally to the waist line (when the second lap began, Julie was definitely too tired for that) and a reach of alternating—right or left—hand.

At the end she was even too exhausted for counting.

"...three...four...five," she was nearly whispering with a hoarse voice.

"Ekku, ekku..." Ivy choked on a sip of water when they were just before the end of the pool.

Julie turned around and pulled her to the starting platform. Ivy was laughing. For a second or two Julie felt in the same way as if they both still were in a duet.

"Good, now let's get down to the figures!" Mia was again close to them. "Everyone, barracuda split till the end!"

Again, a short time without breath, vertical thrust to the maximal height—it wasn't that easy—and finally, the split in the air. At least it didn't hurt after a few years of training.

Julie felt the water line an inch below her hips. Too low, but there was no other option than to do the split. She was able to redo the barracuda for a few times, without going up for the air, until the coach called for the end of the training.

"For the next time, everyone with perfectly knoxed hair, and no hair gel allowed. We won't let you in with it, understood?" Mia was talking about their hair makeup, which was a big fail on the last competitions.

"Yeah, understood," she thought and went for her backpack lying in the corner, next to the speaker and cables.

"Julie, you're gonna take this away!"

Only thirty feet of way back from the pool storeroom, and the easy part of the training would begin.

She took her training stuff and weights and quickly ran ten steps down to the corridor leading to the changing rooms.

The rest of the team was already there. Julie swiftly passed the showers—only Annie and Lexie were still chattering here—and went straight to the lockers.

Vikki, Chloe and Kenzie were taking another nutty photo in the mirror.

"Julie, wanna be in?" they were very busy, but still able to note her presence.

"Okay," she said with more custom than excitement in her voice. She was really tired.

"So go inside, you take the phone!"

After a few really silly seconds she was free again. Another dozen of weird poses would be really fine for her (and Chloe surely sounded like somebody with decent ideas for more funny photographs…), but she was looking for Sophie.

When Julie finally found her on the other side of the changing room, her friend was ready to go, standing in her jacket, with her long, stunning, auburn hair already tied up into a half-braid.

"Are you going to talk with him tomorrow?" Julie asked when Sophie was opening the door.

"Yes, tomorrow…" she said quietly.

"So tell him everything. And don't force yourself to anything."

"Yes, but…" Sophie closed half-opened exit door.

"But what?"

"I feel little sorry for him."

"He will understood. I'm sure he will."

"You are going to catch a cold." Sophie looked at Julie, standing in her swimsuit, still a bit wet. "Thank you."

"Who wanna fight in the ultimate gel-in-a-costume competitions?" Vikki was shouting from the lockers zone.

"Me!" Julie ran back to the changing room. "Till Saturday!" she said turning around to the closing door to the hallway.

After the unofficial changing-room contest, Julie wasn't perfectly sure if winning was worth trading sixty-dollar swimsuit, she probably lost in the sea of chemical reactions between gel, fabric and some mysterious fluids from Chloe's bag, yet the prize had already been given and anything could be changed.

She got out of the pool building. Chlorine was

one of the best smells in the world, but the fresh air was really nice too. Their large sport-ute was already waiting for her at the parking in the darkness of the June night. She opened the door.

"So how was your synchro stuff?" mom asked her.

"All right," she answered.

Mother glanced at her briefly, and then she was again looking at the road as they were leaving the parking in front of the pool.

"Are you preparing that show for the end of the school year?"

"Mom! I told you two weeks ago that we had re-signed from doing it. We have to pay more attention to the technical routines before the—"

"Never mind. I thought it would be a great occasion to show your talent, but okay." Mother was angry. Without a reason, as always.

"But, mom, you don't understand. We are in the middle of the season for—"

"Not keeping up your promises? Not important. I keep mine." She was now looking only at the dark street. "I said we would pick up Lily for the overnight stay and—"

"Surprise!" her best friend suddenly peeped from the front seat. "Eat something!" Lily threw to her some object in a rustling, foil wrapping. "How was your day?"

When Julie caught the cereal bar, she couldn't decide what was more important for her: Lily or the eating. "Good. We haw the eggbeathea for the mosth of the trainingh," she tried to satisfy both needs at the same time.

"With weights both on arms and legs?"

"Yeah." Whole-grain oats with honey tasted really great, no matter how exhausting the swimming fifteen minutes ago was.

"Oh, God. Mia is killing you!"

"And we haw the crawhl with no breathing. I did a few fifties," Julie finished the cereal bar.

"My Julie! You are the best synchro swimmer in the whole world!"

"My Lily! You are my best friend with the sweetest after-training snacks!"

"We are home!" Julie opened the door.

"Jools!" Dad was at home too, always ready to use the nickname she hated. "The school?" Everyday questionnaire had begun.

"Good."

"Swimming?" This question was the middle one.

"Tolerable."

"Hungry?"

"And what do you think?"

"Then the kitchen is yours."

After the paternal inquiry, she was fully ready for the supper. Eating after training!

"Lily, will you try to eat like a synchro swimmer?" Julie asked while opening the fridge.

"Not sure if I'll survive it."

"Won't you try, won't you know!" Julie was setting up two plates at the table.

After emptying a whole bowl of salmon tartare, a can of red and green peppers and two bags of olives, all combined with cumin, thyme and caraway, she still felt little hungry.

"Now the fruits!"

"Julie, are you sure?"

"As much as I'm sure I will be late for school tomorrow morning!"

"You are never on time!" Lily made a face like if she had just seen news about enormous disaster threatening the whole country. "Okay, give me that fruits..."

Four fruity cocktails were already waiting in the

fridge. And some extra, green sweeties were prepared in a basket on the window sill.

"Jools, little preparation for the final exams wouldn't do any harm to you," her father's voice sounded from the living room when she was finishing a watermelon-with-pineapple salad.

"Dad, we are little tired!"

"Just sayin'."

"All right, Julie, let's go upstairs to do the homework," said Lily, only a little suspiciously too loud.

They locked up themselves in Julie's room.

She lay down on her bed with a book taken from the shelf. A map of the United States on a sloped ceiling fluttered a little when her shadow veiled the South, bathed until then in the sun of the halogen desk lamp.

After a minute the book was left on Julie's bed, beneath her arms. "Would you do the same?"

"What?" Lily didn't quite catch the subject as she raised her head from the phone.

"Leave your broken home and go for a journey of a lifetime with your love?"

"Why?" Lily was somewhat puzzled. "Are you

planning something I should know?"

"No, Lily," now Julie was holding the book in her hands again, with the title pointed straight into Lily's face. "I'm asking you about the book! Would you do the same thing as she did?"

"Nah, Julie...! Don't you have easier questions? You are supposed to be tired."

"Yes, I am, but—it's intriguing me. I've just finished reading and I do not know if I would do the same thing as she did." The book was open again. "Sorry for the spoilers, but 'she turned around,'" Julie began reading, "'with her wavy, nut-brown hair raised by the wind, and vanished on the street in the deep shadows of the skyscrapers.' You see?" Julie was shivering with all emotions. "They didn't make it! She got back to her parents. I really don't know if the whole thing was a worthwhile deal. And the name is so similar!" she nearly dropped the book off her bed.

"Oh Julie, I honestly don't know..." Lily put down her phone.

"It has to be so tough to get through all obstacles to that bliss, that paradise, and then resign at the end."

"Shouldn't we sleep a little? It's one o'cl—"

"After all, I wouldn't dare to do so."

"And we didn't finish our homework, not

mentioning the preparation for the exams..."

"And I would find a way to—"

"Julie!"

"What?"

"Life is not a book."

"Wake up, Julie!"

She was lying face upward on her bed. The room was covered by early daylight entering through the second window. It had to be well after the sunrise, yet before the alarm time.

"Are you alive?" Lily was somewhere out of her sight. "You need to hear this!"

"Yeah..." Julie slowly turned her head to look at her friend. She was half-sitting between her bed and the desk, with Julie's phone in her hands. "So what's the big news?"

"You and your team! Qualified for the Summer Olympics!"

For the first few seconds Julie was unable to move a finger or even an eyelid; she nearly forgot to breath. She was still lying in her bed, gazing in the ceiling with her green eyes looking in fact farther away, than at the map of the USA. London, she was going there.

Any from thousands of her bronze hairs spread over the pillow, any from her two raised eyebrows, nor her half-open, little mouth knew what that meant. She only knew that it happens only once in a whole life, to be in the Olympics.

"Wait, there is more..." It looked like Lily was still able to talk. "You got an F in geography exam."

"Oh my God." Julie slowly learned how to speak.

"Don't worry, I got an F too. And besides... you are going to the Olympics."

"No, I'm not!" she was now fully capable of speaking, yet she had no time left for it!

"Are you not going to explain me why—" Lily started talking when Julie was still standing in the room, "you are not goanna dress yourself..."

"Well, that might be a good idea," she was back in the door.

"Well, I'm listening."

"No, later! I mean dressing before the school." Julie grabbed three or four random things from her wardrobe and she was out of the room again.

Lily was in a tornado once. She was five or six, locked with her whole family in a safe room. It was scary, yet far more calm experience than the upcoming morning.

In the middle of the way to the bathroom she run into—or maybe better—was the subject of running into for some blurry, disheveled, amber-haired, half-dressed object in a black sleeveless, which looked like Julie in a great rush.

When Lily was in the bathroom, she heard the series of rapid crashes or even explosions located somewhere below the tiles of the floor.

And when she went downstairs, only the traces were left. Firstly, the single sock. Thick, woolen sock suspiciously similar to the ones worn by Julie. Then, a running tap, pouring the stream of water straight at the pile of olive-colored plates from yesterday supper, making Julie's home more green than ever. With a big hope for additional party, as the emerald waterfall was very close to the switched-on toaster. When Lily went from kitchen to the hall, the sounds of explosions turned out to be emitted from the four drawers thrown away on the floor from a large commode standing in the corridor. However, there was no clear evidence why their presence there might be helpful for Julie. Only after a while Lily thought about her friend desperately looking for the lost sock in them—this could be a good clue.

The front door left wide-open didn't look like a disaster—to the moment when Lily realized that Julie's parents were out for about an hour, her friend somehow managed to get the only key with her and the house had to be abandoned unlocked if she wanted to go to school that morning.

In the middle of a path between the building and the street, Julie's soup plate was standing with a wild mixture of milk and cat grains inside.

Lily saw a kitten slowly sneaking to the bowl. "You watch the house!"

Until now, Julie wasn't aware of her fantastic ability to get up that early and to left the house that quickly. She got by with dressing up, cleaning the dishes from the supper and preparing the breakfast for Lily in just ten minutes! And she even fed the cat and remembered not to lock her friend in empty house. Or maybe... well, she was not completely dressed (where the hell that sock was?), the plates could be treated with a better care (but they should be clean by now...) and the toasts for Lily might be little burnt (she was going downstairs, right?). Anyway, she left the house and was on her way to school. And now she needed a good plan. A perfectly matched, second-to-second plan for the next fourteen days, if she was still going to be in the Olympics.

For the last couple of months she had... sort of... left behind a couple of things. An F in her geography exam meant that she would probably fail the whole subject by the end of the school year. She was ready for fail in physics, but with two fallen classes she wouldn't have the possibility to take a resit in the summer break. Moreover, her biology teacher said he would give her a passing grade only if she pass in geography. And in biology she was near to extinction too!

But that was only the top of the iceberg and the Titanic of her mid-school graduation with allowance for skipping the second half of June to take part in the games, starting this time little earlier than usual, had just started sinking. It was eight or seven minutes before midnight and she needed to fix a hole, raise the ship and turn it back on a path to Great Britain by two o'clock in the morning. Otherwise...

"Julie!"

She turned around. It was Chloe and Kenzie.

"Five to eight!" Chloe shouted again.

"On time for the first time!" Kenzie was also re-ally impressed.

"Hey…"

"We have the games-entry party at Vikki's to-day," said Chloe. "Her parents are out, so…"

Kenzie came one step closer to Julie. "Ariana is coming."

Ariana was the oldest one in their team. She almost never got involved in younger's parties. If she was, it had to be something big.

"Well, I will probably have no time left today… for the party…"

"Why?"

"I have left a couple of things behind…"

"So you don't know yet if you are coming?" Chloe smiled.

"I don't know if I'm coming to the Olympics."

"What?"

"Sorry, gotta go…" She made two steps back.

The main door opened and her best friend, little dazed, entered the school hall.

"Hey Kenzie, there is Lily! She would know what's going on here. Let's ask her."

"Don't do that!" Julie shouted to Chloe and ran along the corridor to the physics classroom.

She ran a lot during the next few days. Breaks were definitely too short to go to all places she needed. Firstly, she had to repair as much as possible in her geography, biology and physics grade lists. Secondly, she got some minor problems in math, little archeological troubles in history, dated as long ago as two months before the end of the first semester, and a big black hole in the middle of her astronomy records. Thirdly, there was a wee attendance crunch in her evidence since she joined the school, so she had to be on time on every class since like now to have at least microscopic odds for any justified leave in the near future. All that sounded feasible to the moment it was no longer only a plan.

At first, she discovered that geography and biology textbooks had a very good reason to be so thick. And that reason was also why her marks were still on the same below-the-sea level, although she had started to read them. "Started," a fair word.

Then, physics turned out not to be the thing she thought it was. The teacher wasn't playing dice and her grades were completely time-dependant in terms of her preparation to quizzes.

At last, while she was taking more and more re-sits in math, history and astronomy, she was falling in more and more attendance problems, as all retake periods took place on other lessons. So she was slowly becoming a better graded, yet hardly present student!

Titanic was fighting with her spare strengths. The stern of the ship was already up and the bow was going down with a great speed.

"Why don't you take one of the advanced placement exams?" asked Lily when they were eating a school dinner together, just in the middle of some very busy day. "You will save a lot of time with that, as they can replace a passing grade for up to three normal-level subjects."

"But I can't get AP in geography nor in biology, cause I'm below the passing average in them already!"

"You have four days to succeed in three classes you have no positive mark since the last semester. Besides, you have daily trainings and half of a dozen other subjects to improve your grades." Lily stopped eating her quinoa salad. "Julie, I really think that getting the AP exam is your last chance if you want to get to the Olympics." Lily's fists were clenched. She looked more serious than ever.

"Okay, you've convinced me. Let's choose the subject."

After a short while bowls after the salad were out, and a large card of classes available for AP exams was laid on the table between Julie and Lily.

"Physics, biology and geography are out for obvious reasons," she started from the top of the card.

"Math is also not a good idea." Julie was looking at the list from the opposite side of the dinner table.

"Then maybe athletics?"

"They won't let me to take this exam, Lily."

"What about gardening? You liked it in primary school?"

"But now I don't."

"Julie, you have to decide for something!"

"Yes, but maybe for the subject I have non-zero chances to pass?"

"Great, so I'm reading the card from top to bottom." Lily's finger went down through the list.

"Pottery?"

"Are you crazy?"

"Programming?"

"I hate programming."

"Poetry?"

For a second or two a shadow of agreement appeared on Julie's face.

"I think poetry is our choice." Lily smiled a little.

"I got C in poetry for the last semester… It's not the best—"

"I certainly think that poetry is our choice." For the second time that day, Lily's voice sounded very convincingly. Julie raised her eyes. Her friend's finger was on the last subject on the list.

Actually, choosing the subject for the advanced placement exam was a lot easier than preparing to taking it. By the end of the first of two weeks left to the start of the games, the frequency of their trainings had increased to the amount barely livable alone. But she had also regular school classes combined with retaking as many tests as possible apart from them. And she was supposed to learn for the poetry exam at the same time? Not possible.

Now her day was starting around six in the morning with a way to the pool for the first training session, from seven to nine o'clock. A seagull was eating a prawn, a flamingo was hunting the seagull and the barracuda was biting them all just before the never-ending reiteration of their Olympic routines with going over and over again through every choreographic section. A whirlwind had been launched.

Then the school. A loony accumulation of end-semester projects, not mentioning negative attendance marks for skipping first two lessons... She had too much classes to do all homework assignments, and simultaneously not enough to retake all tests she failed during the last semester. Once, she had to split one lesson for two overlapping resits from biology and physics. A passing grade was offered from fifty percent of correct answers in each one of them, so why not to try writing a half of each other perfectly and wining them both at the same time? Even air traffic control had to be a breeze compared to that.

And later, at three-thirty, her second daily training was beginning. More eggbeater, barracuda and Catalina, all with four weights on. Why on Earth she was taking them off in the morning? She could save a minute of precious time by not putting them on once again in the afternoon. She was falling asleep while doing a hybrid upside down in the water, yawning when up in the air, dreaming about going sleep earlier than ever in her whole life.

That wild chase with time, mixed with the insane fight for an inch-better height over the water level in heron, was over at half past five. At the end of the day Julie was so exhausted that there was nothing better to do than to feast on a dying ship.

Julie's favorite shop was Warren Decoratives, right on the border between the city and the suburbs. She had been buying there all fancy materials for her suits and headpieces for the last five years. A perfect place for the rest after a hard day.

A little foil bag enclosing a few dazzling objects was the thing that absorbed completely Julie's mind for that moment. Gleamy crystals looked like tiny, lively sparks. Lily was wandering somewhere in the fabric section.

"Julie... As a matter of fact, why we are here?" Apparently she was not that much captivated by the charm of the place. "You will get a swimsuit from the national team, won't you?"

"Yhmmm..." Julie didn't raise her eyes from the shiny miracle.

"So what's the point in looking for suit decorations?"

"I need to make the headpiece for my solo routine on my own," she whispered.

Lily looked at a small package in Julie's hands. "Are you going to buy these?"

"Yeah..." she was still staring longingly at few colorful stones.

"But it's twenty dollars for five crystals."

"And I will need six or seven packs of them..."

"Julie, they are gonna cost you a fortune!"

"It's for a very special occasion..." her hand gripped another few bags. "They are real rhinestones..." she said with a dreamy voice.

"Do what you want. But after all, will you have time for making the headpiece? You are flying to London in two days and tomorrow is the AP examination day—have you practiced for your—"

"We will also need a lot of golden sequins..." Julie put a bunch of rhinestone packs into her basket and quickly dived into the shelves with beads.

"Poetry exam...?" Lily stayed by the crystals.

"And a deep-red needlepoint! Haven't you seen it in the fabric section?"

"Julie!"

She stopped halfway to the sewing accessories and turned around to Lily. "What?"

"The poetry exam! Have you studied for it?"

"Not quite..." she looked somewhere far below the floor. "The schedule was tight..."

"So buy that rhinestones and we—or maybe better you alone—are going home to learn poetry."

"But, Lily, the headpiece?"

"See you tomorrow, after the exam!"

When Julie got to her home, the day was fading. Her room, normally snowy-white, was graying out in the dimming daylight.

Julie put the bag from the shop on her desk. The need for a break started to win with all others, eating included. She was even too tired to make the headpiece. Headphones, phone locked in airplane mode and her bed seemed to be an ideal combination. Julie was between these three objects in less than five seconds.

She was nothing but her resting back, her ears and her music.

In the morning her mind was as clear as the sunny sky above her during the walk to school. She made a fast reconnaissance through all poetry-related themes she was aware of.

The name "Taylor" was somehow connected with something she heard last evening (just before falling asleep in all clothes, with headphones on her head, and not waking up till the morning). She remembered one cool poem by Cummings, although it was pretty obvious it won't appear on the exam (she read it only for herself one sleepless night in a book stolen from the library). She also knew that Annabel Lee was not a girl from her school and that she was dead for a long time (but why and where she died?). The ellipsis might be now her favorite poetry technique.

The first section of the exam was actually about poetry techniques. Julie waded through it by some homeopathic leftovers from the last semester course, diluted in the whole ocean of her illiteracy. At the end, she felt like after some crazy breath-holding for the whole routine. And then was the second part: work with text.

"Diving into the Wreck" was the first exercise. "Theme analysis—find the topics most interesting for you and develop them," read the line right above the title. For Julie the task sounded like "be dead and buried, best time wins," yet she started reading the poem.

> First having read the book of myths,
> and loaded the camera,
> and checked the edge of the knife-blade,
> I put on
> the body-armor of black rubber

In the set of objects from the first stanza, the camera and the book were quite appealing to her, but the knife-blade and the armor felt somewhat disconnected from diving. Maybe after some short thought... Anyway,

> First the air is blue and then
> it is bluer and then green and then
> black I am blacking out

It was intriguing. "Well, you could name the feelings you get from not breathing for a long time in that way," Julie thought before going to the last lines.

> and there is no one
> to tell me when the ocean
> will begin
> THE END OF QUOTATION.

"They cut it off just when it was starting to get interesting!" she thought (and maybe made a slight grimace on her face, as some girl sitting on her right side looked at her a little baffled).

The first task turned out to be pretty easy. She wrote about reading "the book of myths" and "loading the camera" before the journey, then having some troubles, and finally, finding out that she would have to discover the beginning of "the real life," as she put it, by herself.

The second exercise left some choice for her at the beginning. It was the interpretation of a poem, and she got two of them to pick up one to describe. She looked at the authors and titles. The first set read, "'Death' by E. Dickinson." Julie checked the other one. "'There's Just No Telling' by J. L. Knox."

"It sounds familiar..." she said to herself and chose the second one.

The poem was rather sad. The ending almost made her cry (it wasn't true, but she had to add some emotions). That could be a story of some wrecked family or relationship. A dialogue without the real talk. With a bit of luck, somebody might believe in her interpretation.

The last task was probably arranged by the

examiners to be a no-sweat one. Filling the gaps in the last stanza of "The Road Not Taken" by Robert Frost. The problem was that she had never read the poem. She remembered one boy talking once on her poetry class with a great excitement about some other Frost's poem, "Fire and Ice." If the exercise had been an interpretational one, the two-hour lecture would have been helpful. She could veer from the completely unknown poem (her bad attendance marks were closely connected with numerous memory holes in poetry...) to the one she was able to recall something about (the lecture had left a light reminiscence in her mind).

But the task was purely good-memory dependant. The gaps were made in the very end of the piece:

> Two roads diverged in a wood, and I—
> I took the one _____,
> And that has made all _____.

The beginning of the poem wasn't printed, so all chances for any possible clues from it were gone. She had no better choice than trying to make something up.

Julie thought for a while. Had she ever been in a forest, with two roads to chose one? Not really. But what if she had?

The clock over the blackboard was slowly ticking. Other students were quietly preparing to return their exams. Julie leaned over her pages and wrote:

> I took the one less traveled by,
> And that has made all the difference.

After the exam Lily didn't show up. She wrote Julie something about bad cramps and sick leave for the whole day. So she had now around three hours of waiting for the test results. She was sitting by the lockers in empty corridor. Only the advanced placement exams were led at Friday. She had no other lessons nor resits. It was probably a good time to do a little summary of her situation at different school fields.

She opted for interchanging the mark from her AP exam for passing grades in biology, geography and physics. During the last three or four days she left the resits in those subjects completely, and was retaking only tests from math, history and astronomy. And she had improved her marks in them to the state at which her succession wasn't at risk. Attendance marks also were no longer a danger to her. Not a single unjustified absence or late for the last two weeks. If she passed the exam, she would get a school graduation and instant allowance for skipping the rest of June for the Olympics.

Julie rested her back against the locker door. She felt little tired. Why not to take a short nap? She had never slept in school—no, in a school corridor. But sleeping in class—that was another story. Once, she dozed off on physics and dreamed for a while about being on a biology lesson with a parental health as a subject. Then Vikki woke her up for the drill questions. The teacher asked her about calculation of the oscillation period. It was somewhat awkward, but she started talking, being only a little sleepy...

When the fuss was over, Vikki awarded her with a "master of funematics" title for the whole next week! What a story it was...

A school bell woke up Julie not in the exact same place where she fell asleep. She was clasped inside the locker she leaned on an hour ago. Julie slowly got off from this odd place, her arms at first, then the rest of her body.

The locker was closed and probably contained some jacket or shoes when she snoozed. How its owner opened it and pulled out the contents without waking her up? She was glad those questions weren't included in the exam.

"So that's how sleeping in a school corridor looks like," she said and went to the north wing of the school. Her shoulders and collarbones weren't in the best shape ever.

Still a bit dozy, she found the board in the hall where the exam results were supposed to appear. There was nobody around.

She started reading from the bottom of the list. She quickly passed a red line separating five or six unlucky students from those who passed the exam. Her name wasn't on both sides of the border.

Julie started reading again. And again, she didn't find herself on the list. Was she excluded for whatever reason?

A third look on the results. One more time from the low end records. After a split second she jumped to the top grades. A short spark of thrill and bliss touched her neck. She was third with her name printed in all caps next to her impressive score: 90.7 points.

Back at home, when she was lying in her bed, she still couldn't fully believe what happened that day.

An A in poetry exam (not mentioning her mysterious teleportation during her sleep). Third score in the whole school... So she was going to the Olympics. Tomorrow. She wasn't sure if she was happy or sad. She hadn't talked with Lily. They wouldn't meet until she would be back. Be back? How strange would that be? Returning to home after the games.

CHAPTER TWO
The Headpiece

THE WAY TO THE AIRPORT was swell. Two hours in one car with Chloe, Kenzie and Vikki with no coach included. A dream in a dream!

They parked somewhat far from the terminals. Julie got out of the car and stopped her hand halfway to close the door. She saw a fence, a razor wire and a starting plane.

"Oh, great!"

"Don't worry, it's perfectly safe!" said Lexie, struggling to keep the speed Julie was moving with.

They were going through the busy terminal,

pulling their wheel suitcases behind them.

"I hate flying."

"But you haven't ever tried to." Lexie managed to pass two other passengers overtaken by Julie a second ago.

"And that's why I hate it!" She was a mixture of shivers, butterflies and willies.

"I was afraid of flying too," said Sophie. She wanted to calm her a little, but when she opened her mouth again, Julie was already on the beginning of their group.

"Can't we just buy a ticket for an intercontinental cruise?"

"But, Julie, it would take us the whole first half of the games to get to Europe by a ship!" Lexie was once again next to her.

"Besides, remember what happened to the Titanic?" it was Chloe, catching up Julie on the way to the boarding-pass machines.

During check-in she drew the place right next to the emergency exit.

"What does it suppose to mean?"

"Be cool." It was Vikki, who had also finished the check-in next to her. "You will be the first one to jump out of the plane if something happens."

"What?"

"Every passenger gets a parachute."

"Really?"

Vikki's face looked like in-between preparing for the reception of a diplomatic corps and leading the best night party ever.

Julie had to take the whole story for granted. The thought of jumping off the plane 30,000 feet above the ocean wasn't very comforting, but the parachute was some kind of a protection at least.

Security check went quite fast, yet nobody seemed to be concerned about any safety accessories for the passengers. The same thing happened at the gate. Julie gave her boarding pass and passport to the flight attendant and received in return the same set of documents. She looked around behind the gate, in a doorway to a jet bridge.

"Fitting room is fifteen steps ahead." Vikki got through the ticket check just after her.

The floor in the jetway was only a little shaky, like the boarding ladder to the ship. At the end of the long hallway was one, big, steel door. Julie turned around before entering the plane. She didn't get a parachute.

It was two in the afternoon when they landed, but it was hard to say what time it was for her. The clock went eight hours ahead, her flight took another twelve and she didn't sleep at all (except maybe last forty minutes...). So she was probably one day forward and one night back.

First place she saw after flight was the airport. Mostly the same thing as the one she left at home, only slightly mirrored (what a cool idea to change the directions!). They took a train to the center and after a while she was in London.

The whole city lived by the river. All tall and beautiful buildings, colorful ships, lively streets— everything existed close to or in the water. It looked like a half of the world was squeezed and placed in one point. Even the seagulls and the giant warship were there.

As they were going east, along the river, a need of sleep became more obvious for Julie than she previously thought it could be. She was looking with tired eyes, but she wanted to look. A group of high buildings with the tallest, pyramid-ended one, was especially interesting. They had to look amazing at night. Like the bevy of the fireflies.

And then they took the northern-east ride to

the Olympic Park. At the exit from the station, only one arrow, pointing left and slightly up, was showing their way.

"Okay, then. It's left!" Kenzie ran in the entrance to the shopping mall.

The place was wonderful. Dozens of stores and restaurants, both indoors and outdoors, on the narrow streets under the glass roof. The only problem was they were most likely not getting closer to the Park while wandering between the shops. After twenty minutes of weaving through the buildings, they stopped near the pole with a small map. The Olympic Park was right ahead them, at the end of the alley they were heading, right after the crossing with a street. Its name read, "Westfield Avenue."

"Sounds nice," Julie said, and they went farther the shopping boulevard.

When they got out of the mall and crossed the street, three buildings slowly arose in front of them. A stadium, some nutty, serpentine-shaped tower and a giant coliseum.

"That big one is ours," said Vikki.

The Park was amazing. Red-dusted paths between tufts of grass, lakelets and young trees. Like the ancient garden for the noble people of Rome.

They spent the whole evening walking there among the crowds of visitors.

And then was the money on their credit cards from the national representation fund. Maybe not enough for all fourteen days of the games, but doubtlessly enough for a small party just for their own opening.

"So, for the golden ones!" A few, not necessarily low-sugar drinks were in the air for a split second.

Their hotel rooms were probably never the place for such fine celebration. Beds and floor were all covered by the sweets and snacks they bought in the shopping center (the initial plan was to keep unopened goodies on the beds and empty wrappings on the floor, but this very quickly turned out to be difficult to obtain). The curtains were shut (except the ones in front of the large window with a view of the whole city) and the home cinema set... well, there were no silent hours in a hotel, right?

After ten o'clock Vikki announced a night pizza time. It wasn't quite clear if they were spending a dollar and a quarter for one pound, or rather getting pound and twenty-five pence for one dollar, but eventually they made a request for eighty or fifty dollars respectively.

Right before eleven Julie went downstairs to receive the order with a bunch of all their credit cards, just in case of the need for splitting the costs between a few accounts with a sufficient amount of money.

"Who is going with me to those firefly buildings?" Julie asked when she got back to the room with pizza. (It was eighty dollars and she had to use two cards, but it was all right—one of them won't get a public-transport ticket for the second week of the games in the worst case.)

"What?"

Ivy wasn't surprised by the sum of money they had just spent on a few pieces of pie with cheese and mushrooms, but she was rather intrigued by the nickname Julie gave the location she saw during their walk along the river.

"I think she's talking about Canary Wharf." By some mysterious way, Ariana knew the name of the place Julie was thinking about.

"We are going with you!" Chloe and Kenzie jumped out of their beds.

"Me too!" Vikki was already putting on her shoes,

losing a few mushrooms at the same time.

"Annie?"

"I would rather stay..."

"So do I." Ivy was apparently in the middle of some crucial talk with Ariana.

Sophie said something about not feeling good enough for night trips. She was sitting next to Annie, in the corner of the room. It looked like the team was completed.

The way to Canary Wharf was rather complicated. They changed the trains several times, went backwards by a mistake, and probably didn't use their transportation cards with all required readers. Fortunately, nobody checked the tickets.

The next part was even more difficult. Streets on the other side of the river weren't that much frequented, and as well lit as the northern portion of the city. During their walk, they scared a few foxes and went through a very dark park, which looked like the very last place they would visit. But finally they came in the area looking like forgotten, overgrown shore or a cliff of some kind.

Julie pushed away the branch veiling the view.

They saw a flood of light, gathered in thousands of points falling off and staying in the skyscrapers at the same time. And underneath, the river. No, not the river, rather the waving sea or the dark ocean.

"Didn't I say that they are firefly buildings?"

"Charm!" Chloe caught the railing and leaned out as far as she could.

"Now we are here like in home, Julie," said Vikki. She was born in Los Angeles and lived there for six or seven years.

"Going back?" Julie asked.

"No way!" Kenzie didn't even turn her head from the buildings.

The next thirty minutes were the most silent time Julie had ever spent with her friends. Not a single word, only the waves breaking on the shore and the view.

It was around three o'clock in the night when they got back to the hotel. Julie right away jumped to the bathroom to take a shower. When she entered the room again, Vikki was already in the middle of some—supposedly good—fable.

"It's like comparing a cheesecake and a bowl

of cornflakes."

"Oh, wait, wait, wait! That's my favorite subject!" she shouted, being still in the bathroom door.

"We are not talking about eating, Julie." Chloe was newly taken into the plot, so she apparently felt the need for highlighting her recently gained self-consciousness.

"I know, but it's my favorite subject too."

"Anyway, that's how these things work for me when I'm hungry." Vikki's cooking tale was done. It was time for Julie to start her own.

"For me it's more like the whole-grain muesli," she said.

"Mmm, yummy!" Kenzie was delighted.

"I even sometimes get a dessert after the corn-flakes if I'm lucky."

"It's not possible." Vikki was between envy and strong mistrust.

Julie felt the appetite for a little tiff. "How do you know?"

"I just know," her friend was somewhat stirred for a second. "Nobody asks you how do you know the things you say. But maybe I should." Vikki made her sweetest face with blinking eyes. "We all re-member your last-year story, but we don't know all the details..."

"Oh Vikki... You are my cutest story beggar ever!"

The morning was really tough for Julie. Morning? A second day without morning and evening, and the sleep between them. Phooey! She was barely able to stand or talk, and she was starting in the Olympics.

The Aquatics Center became even bigger when she got closer to it. Inside, straight after the gates, was a long corridor to the changing rooms. Julie was going between Chloe, Kenzie and Vikki, somewhat in the back, trying to keep up with them. She couldn't feel her favorite smell yet, so the whole thing had to be enormously big.

At the right side, large, inwardly tilted windows were separating them from the pool. For a second or two Julie slowed down and tried to catch the first view of the arena. Everything was distant and azure. Far away were some diving platforms.

She saw a girl turned back to the windows, right behind the somewhat bluish glass, standing in a star-shining red swimsuit.

"It has started," Julie said to herself.

The changing rooms also turned out to be a few

times broader than she expected. A whole changing village! No question, why she couldn't smell the chlorine in the hall or in the corridor.

Then a few steps, a short hallway, and she was at the pool. A hundred feet to the other side. A few hundred to the roof. Some flags up there. Everything was little reddish or navy blue.

She couldn't stand the desire and turned around. Ten thousand people on the arena. She felt like a gladiator for a while. The moment, maybe a second, worth the whole life before it.

And then, as soon as the team presentation was over, she—along with the others—was dismissed.

All competitions contained some amount of spare time, and it looked like the Olympics had it even in a greater abundance than the national ones. Every contest she had attended consisted mainly waiting. Waiting for the start, for makeup and hair. Waiting for others' routines and for the results. Waiting for a lunch and for a break. They didn't manage to get that nice place, right in front of the tilted windows, for their camping site. Canada or maybe Russia took it. They would probably have to wait for it to open up.

For the first day, they took the place at the left side, right next to the main exit from the changing village. Not that much comfortable and with such a good view as the one close to the windows, but the decks here were much wider than everywhere else she was, so it wasn't that bad. Julie took off her short trousers and spare flip-flops from her backpack.

At the beginning of all competitions, she always had a walk around the pool. This time it took her a little longer than usual to get to the next sector of the deck (and she had to pass over some "no entry" plates a few times...).

Julie looked in the direction of her team at the opposite side of the pool. Vikki was trying to get some starter swim (it was her first-thing-to-do), but somebody cast her out of the water. Annie was practicing some light acrobatics on the land. She was their flyer. A good thing to do for her. Then, Ivy and Chloe were showing to each other some hybrid from the beginning of their team program. Land drilling. She would also have to do it with them eventually.

Around the place, she was standing at, other teams were setting up their camping sites. Why not to try talking in Japanese? She knew a few words. Okay, few. But there was the ultimate language of synchro, wasn't it?

She found some girl in a white suit with a big red

dot, looking little lonely at the bank of the pool.

"Ohayou gozaimasu," Julie started the conversation with words that were supposed to mean "good morning" or something similar.

"Masaka sonna koto ga aruhazu nai yo! Nihongo shaberu no?" Not a single, understandable word. It was the time to begin the talk in synchro speech.

Julie showed a ballet leg: right arm up, left one sticking out parallel to the floor.

"Aaa, balet legu!" Japanese contestant understood exactly what she tried to say. In a response, the girl raised her left arm and touched it with the right hand slightly below an elbow. It was a heron.

After an hour, when the teammates of her new friend gathered for stretching, and the sign conversation came to an end, Julie knew the whole choreography for the Japanese team routine. Quite nice. Hard to beat if they would do it right.

Julie's first performance, a pre-swim of their team program, was planned for three o'clock.

She ate lunch. A chicken with a tomato salad, quite eatable. First portion in the restaurant on the second floor behind the arena, and the next one taken away to the pool. Seconds weren't limited, a good thing. Their team pre-swim got a reschedule to four-thirty. Not a good thing.

In the afternoon all colors shifted to much warmer than they were in the morning. The sunlight has changed.

She started making her headpiece. All materials were in her backpack. There were three steps: cutting the needlepoint for the base of the headpiece, sewing the material to it and then placing the decoratives. But the problem was, how to place them? The whole thing should be at least compatible with her solo-routine swimsuit. Anything above a mere consistency was much appreciated.

Ultimately, Julie cut two long shapes from the needlepoint. All in all, some point to start was better than any.

She felt a little sleepy. Was it allowed to nap during the waiting for a routine at the Olympics? Once or twice she fall asleep during some minor, state-level competitions, but now she couldn't hide from the spectators' sight under any balcony nor terrace, so a snooze was probably not a good idea. She would better get back to the headpiece making. The rhinestones, sequins and a few straps of the golden-brownish fabric were waiting in her backpack. She knew the colors, she wanted to have, but what about the rest?

Fortunately, she would have a lot of time to finish the headpiece design. Their pre-swim performance, as well as all other routines, were shifted one day forward. Yuck!

The next day came really quick. It was true that Julie had helped it by sleeping for all fifteen hours between the end of nearly endless waiting at the pool and the morning, not counting twenty-minute break for a somewhat late dinner around two in the night...

She ate dinner, agreed, but when she woke up, it was too late to eat a breakfast. She had to go straight to the Aquatics Center.

"Hey Julie, catch a sandwich!" Thankfully Vikki still had some money on her card and bought them some snacks. Eating at the pool, she loved it!

The atmosphere became little dense. It was half an hour to their first performance at the Olympics.

Around nine o'clock they were asked to get on the deck. She liked the walk-on and the pre-deckwork. She liked that short little moment before entering the stage too. The moment of uncertainty, of waiting about to end, of pride about to come.

The last twenty seconds. Time to put their nose clips on. Julie did it as the earliest one, the rest followed her in a quiet, harmonious wave.

A light breeze of chill and warmth at the same time. A while that could last forever. She turned around to look at her team. Lexie, right behind her, in the second row, was half-smiled while looking fondly far away; she was in the same state as Julie. Then Chloe with a clenched fist, little too much than it was needed, pressed close to her hearth. Gazing with a sharp sight at the judges. Vikki at the end, slightly lost in her thoughts, not quite ready yet. Her hand in the middle of the way between waiting and posing. Ariana in the back, next to her. Kenzie telling last things to Annie. And in the first line, at Julie's right side, Sophie silently staring in the ground, shyly concentrated.

The opening step of the walk-on. Hard to tell, what was first: a whistle, her raised foot or a drop of water falling from her toe on the tiles. And then they all marched away.

Her back and legs bending into ideal arch, her arms and shoulders tilted like the Eagle Nebula wings. The twilight sunrays in the air before her. She was the leader. Everything behind her slightly back in time after her movements if one could stop them in their walk for a moment.

She was the comet, the falling star, marching with other stars through the deck. A streak of happiness, light and bliss. Getting through the shiny particles of dust floating in the air, like a sheer sparkle of thoughts and dreams traveling across the universe. The turn for the pre-deckwork, whole arena before her, beginning at the edge of the pool just beneath her toes. A first touch of the water. A tail of the comet reaching the hearth of the sun. Glimmers of light mirroring her in the surface. The jump of the living fire being watched by the thousands. Arms up to the sky, a breath of weightlessness, the fall toward the blue, and she was back on Earth again.

A starting hybrid. Insanely fast switching between the crane and the bent knee.

She had nothing but the music and their sculling to tell what was going on up. But judging from them, they were in sync!

After the walkout they were up for a second. All on time. The height was good. Now the next underwater part!

And again, their hands during the sculling were quite decently synchronized. The same should happen with their legs above.

A longer arm section. Now the breathing was starting to be really pleasurable.

And then was the platform lift. A big dive. She set up herself on her position. Chloe also took her place on the opposite side, but for a moment she showed Julie opened hand. Something was wrong. Chloe was out of the lifting.

"Not now, Chlo!" Julie thought. She had to push like crazy to compensate for her from Sophie's right side. Why she had to be strong enough to be traded from base to the lifters?

Finally they raised Sophie, eggbeatering like there was no tomorrow.

Annie hit the surface. Telling from the pose, she was in when falling into the water, she did her thing right.

A pattern change. And the air! She had to force herself a little to go down for the last time. A stack.

"Go Kenzie to that base, we are losing two counts now!"

She did.

And then—no, not the end—but that loony mirror hybrid without a breath before! Crane, bent, crane, times ten! And a sudden stop at the full knight.

From the underwater she saw that the sun went behind the clouds. All rays of light between her arms disappeared.

When she got out, she had large drops of water on her arms and shoulders. Although it was before the results announcement, she knew they had done it. Maybe not their top performance, but something very close to it.

"Julie, I need to talk with you!" Her coach was on the side deck. "Sit," she showed her a row of chairs near the judge panels.

"I'm not that tired."

"Sit, please." Mia's voice sounded really serious.

"Okay, then...?"

"We received a phone call from the national committee. It was about your new birth date."

"What?"

"Listen to Julie, it's gonna be hard, but I will try to tell you it as clear as I can. There was a switch in a hospital when you were born," Mia made a slight pause. "Until now, all what counted was that you were born on December thirty-first, fifteen years ago. But somebody has discovered that the baby born on the last day of the year and then, after spending a night in an incubator, given back to its mother, was not the same. There were two children, first—taken from the mother right after birth, and the other one, returned to her. And you were that second child, delivered to parents in the New Year."

All that didn't feel nice. But in which way?

"They got you by mistake."

That would clear up a couple of things.

Mia was still talking. "Since they don't know your actual date of birth, as well as... the other personal data, your new official birthday is January first, the day they delivered you from the incubator. From now on, you are no longer fifteen, but fourteen years old." She stopped and looked at her. "We tried to contact with your—your... former mother, but she didn't answer the phone.

Julie was speechless.

"We don't know your real name and parents, or your true, exact birthday, but you remain US citizenship."

"Oh, great. What else?" She felt something wet near her eyes.

"As you are now too young to formally start in the competitions, we had to move you to the reserve for your solo and every other routine you take part. But we can't switch you in to change any active representation member."

"So what does it all mean?"

"You can't start in the Olympics, Julie."

In a second, the whole team was around her.

"Gee, Julie, don't cry!" Vikki crouched next to her. "They are watching…"

"Cheer up. You're a year younger than you thought." It was Sophie.

"Yeah, great. But I've lost my family, my home and the Olympics. So, basically, everything!"

"Maybe it's not that bad as you think." Lexie managed to get through Chloe and Kenzie. "Have you tried to call them?"

She stood up from the chair.

"Julie, wait!"

She was no longer a competitor, so she wasn't obliged to be at the pool. She wasn't obliged to do anything!

"Julieee!"

She ran to the showers. Warm water. Waiting for the gelatin to melt and go out from her hair. For the first time she didn't like that moment. Something gooey on her back, the hairs partially stuck together.

As soon as she got dressed, she went to the exit from the Aquatics Center. She needed to be out of it, now!

The Olympic Park was nearly empty. Holding the tears in her eyes, she passed some late visitors. Paths and leaves were wet after the recent rain.

She recalled about the phone. There was no answer. She chose the contact named "Mom" for a few times. The phone remained silent.

She was now in front of some steel, railed bridge. Probably north or south—who cared?—border of the Park.

"Okay, then!" she said to herself and crossed the line between her and the non-olympic part of the city.

The place looked like a big, unused plaza or maybe a parking. A large, long construction straight away and a group of buildings somewhat closer at left. She went toward the buildings. Between her and them was a small river. The plate on the other side read, "Fish Island." She liked fish.

"Oh, Fish Island, give me some luck..." Julie thought when she was entering the bridge.

She felt something in her pocket. The phone!

She tapped immediately the "Mom wrote:" box on a screen.

> I know they have told you.
> It's a very difficult situation for all of us.
> You can take away your possessions
> when you will be back.
> Please don't call me again.
> I would like to find my
> real daughter.

The whole world was lost. She ran ahead, without looking or checking the route. Her tears were everywhere.

Some honking car stopped her a foot or two before the crossing. At her right side were some high frameworks and nearly a dozen cranes between them. New housing development, apparently.

She looked left. Two abandoned, left to wreck, houses. The white text on the brick wall read, "Broken homes."

"Yeah, great," Julie said with the tears in her eyes. "I hate this way!" she shouted so loud that she had to lean for a while before she went straight in the direction of the ruins.

The path turned down just before them. She was at the riverbank. Wilted grass nearly to the edge of the water full of mud and rubbish, gradually turning into a dying swamp. Julie went the footpath along the marsh.

A row of boats at the bank of a canal. Some of them old, worn-out and damaged. The other ones— dead from a long time, the skeletons or bodies slowly decomposing into rust and rottenness. The whole commentary of dreams, swimming a long time ago.

She went through the very dark tunnel and climbed up the steep shore. The air got somewhat colder.

Another bridge. A creek or a canal of some sort. Julie leaned on the railing and looked down. The water was far away. She knew there were two ways of jumping from really big heights...

A breath of mild wind touched her nose, cheeks and mouth fondlingly. She raised her eyes. A single ray of light got through the bed of navy-black clouds. For a second or two she was very, very still.

"Are you really thinking that I can't do it without swimming?" She rapidly turned back and got off the bridge.

The canal, boats, brick walls—all flashed before her eyes when she ran the way back.

It was already getting dark when Julie was crossing the bridge linking the Fish Island with the rest of the city. Far, far away, in a hole between the buildings, she saw Canary Wharf. The pyramid-ended skyscraper was starting to shine over the blacking sky with all its thousands of lit windows.

She felt like in home.

When she entered the Olympic Park, clouds went off a little for the very last part of the day. The Aquatics Center was brownish-golden in the last rays of the sunset. She felt like she was going to her home, for the second time that day.

The upcoming days were really hard for Julie. Her team received 87 points for their pre-swim routine. Probably enough to make a good impression on the games, but not necessarily to qualify to finals and win. The question was, how to change that score into a winning one with such a limited amount of time like less than two weeks? Julie thought a little and the answer also turned out to be the time.

"Are you sure it's gonna work?" Ivy caught her in

the long corridor. "We have never done it that way."

"I think it's the only possible way to do it." She couldn't understand why they were not getting it.

"We are glad you're back with us, but your idea will turn everything upside down," Chloe was very helpful, as always.

Did she really have to repeat all that once again? "I have told you about the winning—"

"We remember the winning without swimming, the ray of light and the sunset you saw, but still…"

"I saw the dead boats too…"

Finally Ariana said they were taking her plan. For a moment Julie thought that they had agreed only because of the compassion for her. But it didn't matter, they had agreed!

Synchronized swimming contained a lot of… well, very subsidiary things, needed for trainings and competitions, but very time consuming. Normally, each one of them did the makeup or dinner in random order, just for herself or for a friend from a duet at best. Not a very efficient way of time management for nearly ten people in the team.

They had a few minor performances in the beginning week. Her routine replaced with Ivy's solo pre-swim (two pre-swims before qualifications in one competition, what a luck!). Then, Vikki's and Kenzie's duets and, if she remembered correctly, some technical routines for all of them. But the most important one was their team preliminary in nine days. Since the last change of the rules, all was dependent from its result: their duets, combination, even Ivy's solo. The team preliminary score would be added to each one of them. And to make things harder, if the team routine didn't appear in the finals, they would not be able to qualify to them with any other routine! She truly hated the new rules (but she had to admit they had changed the name of the sport to the proper one at least). Nevertheless, let's suppose that they wouldn't get a final-qualifying score in the preliminaries... And with their 87 points for the pre-swim performance it was likely to happen.

If she did the dinner for the whole team, this could save them about an hour each day. The makeup was worth around half an hour. For each competitor. Moreover, doing it first for soloists, then for duets, and at the end for the rest of the team would probably allow for additional ten to twenty minutes of training instead of waiting for each one of her friends. They could end a day with two or three hours of spare time, assuming she would do all backup things for Ivy, Chloe, Vikki and the others. Except the performances, which took place a few times per day at the beginning, and then were concentrated at the very end of the Olympics, the pool was open for all contestants to practice...

How much they could correct in an hour per one competitor? Julie clearly remembered that crazy inch of more height achieved during ten days of intensified pre-olympic training, four hours in each one of them. So it was about two-hundredths of an inch of improvement in every sixty minutes of their work. And how was this translating to scores for their team routine...? The calculations were starting to be too time consuming. And Julie's help quickly became inevitable.

"Julie, the eye shadows!" She was in the middle of flipping the whole slew of pancakes and Vikki was in urgent need for makeup for her technical.

"Ten minutes!" she yelled back.

"I was scheduled with my makeup for a dinner time!" Kenzie's voice answered her through the half-opened kitchen door.

"All figures! I forgot they are in a duet!" Julie said to herself. "Hold on, Vikki!" she shouted. "I will be in a sec to finish your eyes!"

All pancakes were on the other side. Four minutes till the end of cooking. Finishing Vikki's eye shadows shouldn't take more than three. She didn't have the time, but she had a sense of it at least!

When she got back, the pancakes were only a little too brown. She had to change the menu. Maybe a salad or a fish? Pancakes were easy to cook, but not in this quantity!

Julie started setting the table. One of the pancakes slipped from the pan and fell on the floor.

"This one will be for Vikki," she thought.

The dinner was ready.

And then was the knoxing. The procedure was as follows.

At first, she had to set the water for the gelatin and empty the whole bunch of Knox envelopes into a cup. Then, if she had already prepared the comb, brush, bobby pins and the hairnet (it could happen from time to time, assuming they weren't lost anywhere hard to find), she was ready to make the synchro bun. Brushing the hair without an end. Tight and smooth ponytail. A braid or two, depending on the hair type.

Wrapping around was the next one step. Five fingers above the hairline, check. Bobby pins to secure any loose hairs. The hairnet at the end. The bun was ready.

In the meantime, the water had boiled, so she could start gelling right away. The nice thing was that she had already some practice with choosing the right proportions of Knox and water, so the gelling wasn't ending in a great mess just before it actually started. First layer combed-in. Second one—painted on. Done.

The whole thing took her about fifteen minutes, or maybe twelve if she was in a rush. She rather was. When she was knoxing the whole team and the first person done by her—usually Vikki—would knox the other one and so on, eight competitors were ready in less than an hour. It was somewhat like powers at match... Earlier, without that gelling management, knoxing for the team routine was taking them around two hours and a half. Ninety minutes of saved time!

So now they were at the point where no precious minute was wasted. But still, there were some problems with their routines. In synchronized swimming lots of points were given for perfection of the performance. The execution was worth thirty percent of their final score. And although their routines were starting to be much better, they were still somewhat far from perfection.

It was something strange with Vikki's legs during splits, Ivy's boosts could be better, and Lexie had a little problem with losing her left leg when doing a double on certain occasions. Chloe was falling on a spin (they all had known about it for ages and that one was easy to correct), and her flamingo wasn't very encouraging (that thing was new and Julie didn't know exactly how to name it). Regarding Annie, there was not much to say about her hybrids or arm sections, she was a silent, competent swimmer—but in the highlights, as a flyer, she needed more energy. Similarly for Sophie, Julie couldn't complain about her figures and movements, they were excellent, yet she had a vague impression that her friend is slightly behind the others (strange thing, it didn't happen if she was counting or during the land drill—the loss of sync showed only when they were swimming to the music). Kenzie's catalarcs were the common issue. Even Ariana's figures were not that perfect either.

It wasn't just the need for more height or more sharpness (which were always welcome…), but some small mistakes not easy to define. And telling precisely what should be corrected was not the only one hard thing. Sometimes even seeing it accurately was difficult when the figure like barracuda was performed with blazing speed by all eight swimmers at the same time. Combined attention of fourteen or fifteen judges might be enough to catch all mistakes when the whole team was in the water. But she was alone when watching her friends' routines.

Julie managed to slow down the time and gather more of it for the trainings, but now she needed to freeze it...

She was sitting high up, at the scene, watching their team routine for the fourth or fifth time and trying to find all possible errors. In a minute or two she would have to go down and tell Vikki, Ivy and others what was poorly done.

She was closing her eyes for short moments and trying to see the pose of the flyer captured for a second or two in the afterimage. Not much time! And then, a short spark of thrill and bliss in her neck.

"Photography!"

Fortunately, Sophie had a camera. Not her own camera. And a very expensive one, by a chance. It took a while to convince her to borrow it for photographing their routines.

"Julie, are you sure we have to do this?"

"I said, there is no other way."

"Maybe we could use your phone—or better mine, I have twenty-eight mega—"

"Do we want to win?"

For a second Sophie looked little frightened. "But you remember what my dad said?"

"Yeah, 'if anything happens to that piece of glass and metal, its remains will form the whole galaxy of sorrow and grief with a death hole in the middle of our house.'"

"It was actually a black hole..."

"Heard, memorized, understood. Can I get it now?"

And at the end was her swimming suit. She had a full schedule of time-saving activities, a camera, a plan to cure their routines, and she had to wear something. Of course, she could put on her shorts and a black sleeveless top she usually wore when being in a reserve or while having a dry day during competitions. But...

Golden sequins at front, coming down in one, and then in two streaks till very behind area.

Dozens, hundreds of them. The sea of brilliant, light-touching, fiery-waved, black stripes, also running to the back, yet little higher, and expiring in two triangular, sharply ended smudges. The background was red-brownish, exactly in that color she liked the most. Backless style, the neckline at a very comfortable height. Downward-pointing, coral triangle just below it, made from different, checkered material. The neck strap was sometimes curling annoyingly, but it wasn't a big trouble.

From the front she looked like an eagle shading its eyes with large, dark wings, and like the head of a giant snake, a viper of some sort, from the back. First effect was surely intended by the suit designers, the second one probably not. But Julie couldn't help the impression of a snake jaw since she saw the photo of herself done by Vikki a few days before their departure.

How could she not wear it? No way! She wasn't swimming, but hey, one thing at least... She decided to put on her solo-routine swimming suit every time she was with her friends at the Aquatics Center. It was sometimes little awkward to go star-gleaming, mermaid-looking to the pool shop for snacks or additional Knox envelope (and dressing up was taking three or four minutes of their valuable time), but she still felt like being a part of the performing team. She even wore it for her first photography day.

She was sitting in a taken-out sector of the scene, reserved for the Olympic crew. Julie was there for the first time since the beginning of the games. But, what was more important, she was holding in her hands a jillion-bucks set of camera, lenses and a few other things she didn't know for sure what they were for. The whole setup oughta take really good pictures!

She set the mode dial on a very promising, green-colored rectangle.

"Creative auto mode. Don't bother with thousands of switches and start making photographs," read the text on a screen.

It was exactly the thing she needed! Now she was ready for photographing. Watching the pool through the viewfinder wasn't the most comfortable activity in her life, although it was probably the thing she would get used to. She found her friends down there, in the water, at the left side of the pool. They were preparing to the team-routine test swim. It was the time to start her job.

The shutter was clicking in a funny way every time she took a picture. Little loud, but it wasn't a bad thing. Much more intriguing were those yellow, shiny dots all over the frame, blinking randomly every time she touched the shutter-release button.

Julie turned the scroll all the way till the end.

"Whoa!" There was a movie option included. It was even better than taking photographs. And could be more helpful for her team.

Two semi-transparent, gray rectangles appeared on the screen around the waving, somewhat greeny water. Annie, preparing to the stack, was in the center of the frame. Julie pressed the round button next to the white icon of a snyc slate, exactly the same thing she saw on the sets of the big movies. A red dot in the upper right corner. She was filming!

After fifteen minutes she had a good collection of short and long shots. A bit of a nice play for her!

Kenzie and Vikki finished their duet. A minute or two to catch a breath before the next routine. It was a good moment to check her work. Julie sat on a chair. She had to figure out how to turn on the review mode. Maybe the button marked with a blue arrow? The screen went all black. Julie pressed the button again. Not a bit better.

She turned around. Somebody was looking at her. A boy with a camera. He was in the press sector, six or seven rows higher than she, alone behind the glass railing, photographing their practice. He might be a few years older than she.

Why he was staring at her? She wasn't the actual swimmer. Or maybe... She was in her competition suit. That had to draw a lot of attention outside of the water, at the scene.

Well... she felt like looking at him for the short time. She turned back again. He was watching something on the screen of his camera. Did he made a picture of her when she was turned away? Did she look good? She touched her nape. The neck strap was curled. Again!

She hadn't prepared her hair. Three minutes for getting in her swimsuit weren't a problem, but there was absolutely no time for knoxing the additional, non-swimming head. Julie's hair was waving loosely on her back and shoulders. A good thing or a bad thing?

She looked around again. He was peeking from time to time at her while putting his photography stuff into a large bag. It seemed very likely that he was going to do something. Something involving her!

Julie didn't know very well what that to do. Should she wait for him? They would have a talk together, wouldn't they? Would he ask her out? It was called "a firstie," wasn't it?

Down, at the pool deck, they were probably waiting for her.

Her pictures! Were they any good? Sophie should know the way to put them on a screen. And what if he would ask about them? She raised her eyes from the floor below her feet. The boy with a camera was already in an aisle between the seats.

"Later," she thought and ran from the scene to her team with her first photographs.

The pictures weren't exactly like Julie was expecting.

"This one is somewhat blurry..." Vikki was the first one to tell what she was thinking.

They were looking at the screen of the camera in her hands. A hazy, creamy object was supposed to be Kenzie in the first phase of Catalina.

"I've told you she lacks some sharpness." Julie was very satisfied that her earlier complains had now very clear evidence (okay, "clear" was not the best word in that case...).

"But look at the water. Those waves and drop-lets are also some kind of misty. I don't think Kenzie is unsharp to that degree," Lexie still wasn't quite convinced.

"Lex, this is the artistic impression!"

"And the colors are little strange too..." Vikki very quickly found another thing to complain about.

Next few dozens of photographs raised similar comments. As the series of cloudy, somewhat faint pictures was getting to the end, Julie saw the signs of boredom in the eyes of her friends. They were look-ing like very eager to go for another training session.

"Wait, I have also the movies!"

But nearly ten minutes of watching didn't help a lot. True, the silhouettes of her teammates were at least not blurred, but everything—their boosts, stacks and floats—vanished in a giant waterquake.

"Why are you waggling the camera during the shot?" Vikki had another difficult question.

Julie had to admit that her movies contained more unintended artistic impression than actually usable information about the errors in their routines. Or even better, about their routines in general...

"Don't be disappointed, Julie, but..." Chloe started talking in a very gentle way, quite unusual for her.

"I believe we all think you have to practice some photography," Ivy slowly finished the long sentence.

Some additional time for making photos might be a good idea, especially if *he* was going to be there again. And Julie felt most likely he would.

"No worries, I will certainly get some practice." She smiled in a most convincing manner she was able to.

"Julie, what happened up there?"

"Nothing." This time her smile was probably not that much innocent as she hoped it to be.

The schedule of their performances had become less dense, so Julie somehow managed to add a self-driven photography course to the list of her daily activities. Besides, she had built for herself a decent plan with everything: knoxing, cooking, watching the routines and helping her team from the land during practices. Now she was starting a day with a quick breakfast for all of them. Then was the gelling and makeup for the ones who had routines in the morning session. Next, a short training. Right after one o'clock, the dinner cooking and knoxing of her teammates scheduled for the afternoon (if anybody). Another practice meet, longer than the first one. At the end, when her team was still in the water, she was starting making the supper. The clock was ticking, but she was fighting.

She stopped wearing her swimsuit. Two minutes to put it on, another two to take it off—it was too time-consuming in the long run. Too bad she couldn't show herself in it, yet those extra couple of minutes were so nice to have that she had to resign from it. Now she could start the first knoxing with some spare time at the beginning, or left the Aquatics Center a little earlier after the last training session.

Vikki and Ivy passed their technical routines with good results. Apparently she was a little too fussy with her complains about legs and boosts, as their scores were not far from the top ones. Other technicals weren't that wonderful, yet they were all in the game so far. Lexie was trying very hard to put more attention to her left leg. And it could be only Julie's imagination, but it seemed that Chloe's spins became slightly better. They were still before their team preliminaries; nevertheless, all that combined with their new training strategy looked like having non-zero chances for the finals.

And as for the boy with a camera... Maybe it wasn't such a "nothing" what happened on her first photography day, but the word was without a doubt accurate for the present situation. He didn't show up for the second time. But it was probably a good thing. She could concentrate on her photographs.

The first thing she had to correct was sharpness. It took her a while to understand that it consisted of two elements: a focus of the image produced by the lens (it was probably one of the reasons why it had so many movable rings) and the time used for capturing the photo (they called it "a shutter speed" everywhere). She decided to struggle with the latter one at first. It was better not to touch that wacky stuff at the front of the camera.

Julie set the scroll on the white letter M (Insanely encouraging message on a screen: "Advanced photographing. Don't use this mode unless you are a highly-trained professional.")

She laid her finger on a shutter dial and started turning it gradually in the direction of greater speeds. It was working! New pictures were less and less blurry. But at the same time, they got darker and darker, until the screen went completely black.

The camera guide said, "If your photographs appear too dark or too bright, use the first ring on the lens barrel to set the right aperture." Arghh! So she eventually had to touch that weird gears on the lens.

The first ring... She tried to turn it a little into right. A nice click. The new aperture was set. Quick look into the viewfinder and another photo. Nothing better. So maybe the other direction?

On her next photograph appeared some ambiguous shadow. Julie got to the end of a scale engraved on the ring very quickly. The last picture was still very dim.

Another dive into the guide. "If your pictures are still too dark, it's time to crank up the ISO speed." Gee! Another thing to care about! When she finally found the right dial, she quickly sat the highest possible number from the list. An instant leap from the darkness to the midday!

But something still was wrong. The whole photograph was covered in a snowy dust. She couldn't even recognize her friends! Any advice from the camera guide?

"Save the extreme settings for low-light situations only. They increase the noise in the image."

A second view on the list. This time she chose some option from the middle. A completely dark frame. Okay, not this one and not the highest, so probably something just close to the top. The brightness improved, but snowy dust was back. Too high!

Julie set the medium value and slowed down the shutter speed. The picture had perfect brightness, but it became hazy again. Any further help?

"Learning correct exposure can be little tricky at the beginning." No fooling!

Julie was shifting all three things desperately for the next thirty minutes. Finally, when the image was both sharp and bright, she stopped at the settings displayed on the screen: "1/4000s, F2.8, ISO 3200." One four-thousandth of a second! They had to be really fast in the water if she needed to use such a short shutter time to capture their figures without blurring.

It was nearly the end of their afternoon practice. Time to get off from the scene and run to the hotel to prepare the supper. It took her five hours to figure out how to take one correctly-exposed picture!

After the supper, in the evening, Julie had a little free time. She started making the headpiece again. But not for herself, as she wasn't the performing competitor. It was a present for Ivy. A surprise. New headpiece for her solo in the finals, if she got there.

The project was uncompleted since the very long first day of the games, she spent at the deck of the pool. Julie tried to recall what she was thinking about at the end of that lengthy waiting. She decided for splitting the headpiece into two elements. Initially she thought about leaving some parts of the red needlepoint uncovered. Ivy's solo swimsuit had at front the same triangle of coral, checkered material as her costume, so not completely hidden fragments of the scarlet canvas could be a good idea. But her friend's suit was a bit brighter than hers. She would probably have to use more rhinestones than she previously thought. She had also those stripes of golden-brownish fabric. So maybe all of them should be used in roughly equal quantities? The golden sequins had to go on the borders, that one thing she knew for sure.

The needle went somewhat tough through the canvas. How long ago she was sewing the headpiece for the last time? Probably ages ago... She was thirteen—no, not thirteen, twelve years old. What a mess with that new date of birth! Now she would have to shift all her memories one year back in time. Good thing, she wouldn't need to exchange them...

Nevertheless, sewing seemed to be easier two

years ago. She would need some time to get back in shape. Meanwhile she would think about the rest of the design. Then gluing the decoratives, and the wiring for bobby pins at the end. She should be done in a few days...

"You can't tell it's not a progress." Vikki was looking on a perfectly sharp, ultra bright photo of a headless flyer in the middle of a stack lift, standing on... well, presumably on the shoulders of the base, cut off by the lower border of the frame.

"Julie..." Lexie's voice was a bit quieter than usual.

"Yeah, I know. I have to do something with the framing."

She left her team on the deck and went to the scene. Hopefully she would find another useful tip in the camera guide.

"There is no short answer how to frame your subjects correctly. Sometimes it takes years of practice." Really? She didn't have years. Hours. A day at most.

Her phone! A few typed words and another search. "Framing is a complex and very sophisticated problem. No set of rules exists for solving this issue."

Julie was heartbroken. No help at all! But... Every

kind of thing had to have some rules. Synchronized swimming and photography framing as well. And obviously she was doing something wrong.

She leaned on the railing. Down there, in the water, they were repeating some lift from the middle of their team routine.

Julie raised the camera to her eyes. There was no other option than to figure out what mistake she was making.

She tried to catch the flyer and base of the stack in a peak moment of a lift, the exact same thing as the last time when she was photographing. A look in the viewfinder, swift touch of a shutter button and a quick review of the photo. She completely missed, it looked identically as the one she showed Vikki and the others.

Her team was preparing to the stack once again. Another attempt with the same result.

She tried to recall the time she was a base. First, she was going down to make place below the surface for the flyer. The feel of some slightly unbalanced weight on her shoulders. Then, when the lifters were just in the middle of their job, was that urge to stand very quickly, but she had to delay it... The delay! There had to be the delay between pressing the shutter-release button and the actual picture-capturing! She was taking the photo at the right time, but the camera—not. That was why she was always ending up with the photography of Annie in the middle of her flight and Kenzie submerging just below the border of the frame.

So now, all what she needed to do was the opposite thing to the one the base had to. Simply taking pictures a little earlier than what seemed natural.

First try. In the viewfinder she had the whole team going down before the next lift. A second of nothing but ripples on the water. Annie's head on the surface. That was the moment of temptation for the base—time for a picture! A click of a shutter and a second later, when the photo appeared on a screen— she had it. Exactly the right pose! Now she could start working.

Eventually, the thing turned out to be not just as simple as taking the picture a split second before she initially thought the right moment was. Sometimes she had to move the frame into a place, where actually no swimmer was (but appeared there at the time the photograph was captured) or set a somewhat wider shot with the zoom ring, because the whole thing took a little more space when fully performed (she was starting to get all those strange things on the lens…). But the overall rule was always the same: be ready for the upcoming move.

Julie gathered a good collection of shots with the whole patterns, stacks and single figures, and ran downstairs to her team.

"Gee, I don't believe my legs look like this!" Ivy was somewhat startled when Julie showed her one of the pictures she took fifteen minutes ago.

"Quite a nice shot, Julie," said Sophie.

On her next photographs they discovered Kenzie and Lexie piked just in the moment nobody was expecting (it was one of the random photos she made to practice framing) and Chloe's legs slightly tipped back (this one Julie took deliberately to prove there was something wrong with her flamingo).

Her photographs started to be a usable help. But now she had to assist her team with the next matching session of their team routine.

All her friends looked a bit unstretched. Not a good point to start the whole thing.

"Reach!"

"But, Julie…" Vikki had always something to say.

"I think there is still a little space to go."

"I can't go further!" This time Vikki wasn't looking like joking.

It seemed that there was a need for some additional stretching. She would have to fit somehow those extra hours into her schedule... For now they had to start with not-so-perfect flexible Vikki.

First hybrid. Not so good as she thought a few days ago. The crane wasn't tipped at the right angle in most cases. A series of corrections. Vikki telling something about being too picky.

Probably it was the time for another move from that section. "Next!"

One of the verticals was definitely tilted forward. "Kenzie, on your face!"

Julie thought that it had to be strange to listen to the commands she was giving to her team. What a jumble it could be if somebody actually heard what she was shouting. Anyway, time for another corrections.

"Lexie, move in!" The pattern was still imperfect. "Second line, keep your windows!"

At the end, when they got to the last section of their routine, Julie watched them all performing it to her counting. The overall image had improved, but it was still not quite ideal in terms of timing. A slight synchronization error.

She got the whole team out of the water and started land drilling the whole routine. The same thing again! She felt like they were still missing something. A split second too fast or too slow.

Julie looked at the opposite side of the pool. The team from Japan was also practicing. She was watching them for the next two or three minutes, peeking from time to time at Vikki and Kenzie swimming their duet nearby. The synchronization at the Japanese side was significantly better than the thing she could see close to her. Why? It was probably the time for a short visit.

Finally they got their camping site near the tilted windows, so she had to go all the way around the pool to get to the part of the deck occupied by bags, clothes and makeup stuff belonging to the teammates of her Japanese friend.

She found her in the water, right next to the edge. Somehow she had to begin the conversation. Should she ask directly about their synchronization method, or try to find it out by herself?

"Sakin dou?" The girl from Japan had noticed her already. Now she had to start the conversation anyhow!

"Hai!" she said. It was one of the last Japanese words she knew.

"Hisashiburi desu!" Her friend was very enthusiastic. She could forgot about asking for help with synchronization. She wouldn't understand a word from the answer...

After fifteen minutes of talk combined with observing and listening to all what was going on in the water, where the rest of the Japanese team was training, Julie knew the magical thing. The language. Shorter words. The difference was small, but it definitely existed. It was called "a millisecond" or something like that on her physics lessons.

She tried to count to eight in Japanese. Then in English. The first language was significantly faster. The delay, exact same thing like in photography. But here, the shorter delay meant less time wasted for spelling and hearing the number, and more of it for doing the choreography belonging to each count. She would have to teach her team some Japanese...

During her way around the pool back to their camping site, Julie came up with another idea. A nice trick, which could show her who really knew the choreography with its counts, and who was watching others for help.

She set the whole team off-pattern, eyes-closed on the land.

"And now you are telling us you will be counting in Ja—"

"Ichi!"

After the fourth iteration of foreign-language, eyes-shut drill, Julie knew everything. Ivy was always a half-count forward, Kenzie had a little need of synchronizing to the others by using not only her memory, and Lexie should pay more attention to the in-hybrid pattern changes. A complete set of corrections. And she managed to get it before the dinner break!

In the afternoon Julie could get back to photographing. The next thing she had to improve were the colors.

Of course, nobody—except Vikki at the very beginning—told her about the problem with colors in her pictures, but the photographs should be nice and neat anyway, right?

Fortunately, this time the camera guide was much more helpful. "For accurate color rendition use the white balance settings. Image sensors record the light differently than our eyes do—even sensors made by various companies can largely differ in terms of sensitivity to particular colors, hence the need for adjusting manually the color temperature for a given scene, time of the day or for artistic purposes."

The whole idea was startling. So there were no true, universal colors? Did every different camera see the light in a different way? What about human eyes? Could the colors seen by Vikki be unlike the ones she saw? But her friend was the one who pointed out the greenish cast on her first pictures... Anyway, in the camera menu was a new option she had to try out now...

She started to care about the right white balance. The next extra element to consider while photographing, but it wasn't such a big problem for her. It was just another small detail to keep in mind, exactly the same stuff like pointed toes or a smile when she was performing the routine and had to think at the same time about a whole bunch of things other than choreography or pattern changes.

The list, which she could display with the

color-temperature button, contained about thirty numbers, the lower ones were to use with artificial lighting and at the sunrise or the sunset, the higher ones—for the midday sunlight or for photographing things covered by shade.

And as soon as Julie got used to setting the right one of them before photographing, she started to realize what she was really seeing with her own eyes. The warm rays of the sun at the pool in the morning. Somewhat bluish, icy light around the noon and all things getting little golden in the sunset. Didn't she notice that earlier? When she carefully thought, she could recall greeny or maybe a bit bluish lighting at their pool at home, similar to the lights they were turning on in the evening in the Aquatics Center. The cold breath of always gray, cloudy shadows... Or the yellow glow of her desk lamp. So the light really was not such a simple thing...

Now all photographs she made were the parts of a very special collection to her. She had Vikki performing splits, a few series of Annie jumping off the lift and Ariana's perfect spins, but she was still missing Sophie in her duet highlights. Ivy swimming her solo would be also a good thing to have. And what about the other teams and their routines?

Julie began to bring the camera for all competition sessions. She was enjoying those little puzzles with choosing the right angle or focal length. It was becoming not only the task of capturing the routines or figures for a reference for her friends, but also some kind of pleasure or a sport for her.

She started to like photography. She started to like taking pictures because they were pictures.

The coking was another thing Julie started to like. Or maybe better—she got used to it. Fixed day schedule with a few extra minutes saved by not getting into her swimming suit made the part of a difference, but the thing which helped at most was probably the change she made in the menu. Now their main, day-to-day course was a salmon tartare. It was easy to prepare and didn't require any cooking in fact! True, the fish was far more expensive than the pancakes, but by some miracle there was still some money on Ariana's credit card.

First thing she was doing after getting to the hotel at the beginning of the dinner break, was taking out of the fridge the chopped salmon, she prepared in the morning. The lemon juice, apple vinegar and a few spoons of oil were already mixed-in. She had to add about a half of a soy-sauce bottle (she was doing nine portions including her own!) and then peel the avocados and tomatoes. A whole bunch of them! They were buying avocados in quantities making quite a stir in the supermarket. Good thing, it wasn't far from the shopping mall to their hotel in the Olympic Park.

After fifteen minutes of peeling, chopping and mixing, the food was almost ready. A while in the fridge, a drop of yogurt sauce for a tasty decoration, minced chives on the top, and Julie could call for dinner.

The dish was yummy! Only Chloe was constantly saying something about not being loons, but she had no other choice than to eat it if she didn't want to be hungry. And after all, how one could not like fish?

The colors of the dish on a plate, lit by the noon sun, were actually similar to the ones Julie saw at the pool. The fish—amber red, nearly the exact same shade Lexie's swimsuit was. The drips of white, creamy sauce like coruscating, pearly tears of stars all over the costume. Bluish edge of the plate, shining with the same, yellowish cast as the azure water touched by the afternoon rays of the sun.

Julie quickly noticed that the whole competitions were composed with three basic shades. The golden glow of joy and satisfaction. Brilliant shine covering all moments of great effort combined with bliss, like the peak of a successful lift. Hard work and practice were always between green and navy blue. Those colors began to appear on her photographs.

She had a very nice double portrait of Vikki and Kenzie stopped in the highest point of the boost in the middle of their duet routine. Their hands joined over the heads, their bodies tilted in the choreographed pose, thousand of water droplets between them and the lens. A whole nebula of particles of water dust, some of them white or silver, others gray and navy, suspended in the air around two lively, yet motionless souls.

Vikki in the front was the one with the triumphant face, chin slightly up, eyes frozen in a conquering gaze. Kenzie in the back posed a bit differently. Looking straight into the lens while getting ready to a dive, raising her eyebrows in a hawkish way, she had a sharp sight of a young eagle.

Some time after taking the photo of Kenzie and Vikki, Julie managed to catch Sophie in her best part of their combination routine. She was on the surface, bent in an angel arch, immersed in the shallow depth of field, drifting in the middle of a golden haze of blurred water swirling around her. Pure happiness on her face. She was dreaming. Her mouth half-opened in the breath of freedom. Her eyes in-between smile and longing, nearly like if she was looking from the Earth at some other, slightly better world.

And finally, she got a photo of Ivy swimming her solo. The greeny cast on the water, two waves breaking and spreading before her friend. Ivy looking beyond the border of the frame, persistent and re-solved, almost stubborn in her firm moves and in her stare fixed at the point where usually the judges were. Everything was sharp and clear-cut, perfectly focused from the left edge of the water trail, through Ivy's arms and profile, to the white smudge behind her.

It wasn't easy to take those pictures. Photographing. Rather a tiring pursuit than a peace-ful look. Sometimes she had to lie on the deck to get the angle and the view she wanted. She was sneaking between other teams on the land, waiting for ages in very awkward positions and taking a series of three or four photos to finally chose only one of them. Not mentioning she got splashed a good number of times.

She was "catching the light" as she was calling it. The hunt for the very best possible sunrays coming through the south windows, showing up between two and three o'clock, the only time in a day to get it. The waiting for the right combination of waves, bodies and the spirit in her friends' eyes. A short fight with sharpness, and then the decisive moment of pressing the shutter button when the image in the viewfinder was a half of a heartbeat before the ideal one.

Julie was just after such hunt for pictures, sitting on the scene, between the lenses laid on the nearby seats, reviewing the photographs she made a few minutes ago and looking at the sparkles of light reflecting on the water. A while of stillness and quiet.

She was starring at the sun glitter on the other side of the pool when she felt a tickle on her nape. She turned around and she saw him.

The boy with a camera. He was back. In the same place as then, when she saw him for the first time. High, over all rows of the reserved seats, in the press sector. And exactly just like then, he was alone, photographing their practice and looking at her between the shots.

She wasn't in her competition suit. Ordinary looking girl. True, in the middle of an empty scene, but the ordinary girl in a black sleeveless top and shorts still. So he had to be really interested in her.

Julie tried to seriously think about him. Was she really into? Yes, she was. He might be interesting—no, he was interesting. She could wait for him or maybe even get a few rows up to be closer. But... There was a slight problem with the schedule. That day was different than a few earlier ones. The second turn of competitions was slowly starting. Lexie, Sophie, Annie and Ariana had their first free solos in the afternoon series of performances. In five minutes she had to be down, on the pool, to show the latest mistakes captured on her photographs. Then, knoxing of a half of her team. And in the end, the stretching with Vikki. She had been trying very hard to put it in their daily plan and it was the only possible place for it. If she was supposed to do everything on time, she had to go.

The boy was clearly observing her. She had the camera full of great pictures. Her hair was gathered in a short, single braid, with a wavy bangs at the front. Not bad. She could be likeable. Only a few steps and he would be down, next to her. Only a few words and they could be setting up their first date. Only a few minutes and she would be late for everything!

"Do not engage!" A sharp thought on the top of others. Something inside her hurt a lot. Something very close to the hearth. Sophie, Annie and others were probably already waiting.

So she really was supposed to lose it? How did one do it? Leaving the most promising adventure of one's life because of responsibilities. Knoxing, stretching and all that stuff. For how long would it hurt!

Julie peeked in the direction of the press sector. She wasn't sure, but it looked like he smiled to her. For a moment she was standing undecided, with the camera bag half-put on her shoulder, between the seats and the exit from the scene.

"Do not engage, do not engage..." her thoughts were jumping between the speeding up beats of her hearth.

Probably she was looking very funny, standing still in the aisle in the middle of the scene, sweating and gazing somewhere in the air. The boy started to put his things into the bag. The whole routine was repeating. So he might be there again! Maybe tomorrow?

"Sorry, not today!" she said to herself and ran downstairs.

The knoxing didn't go as smooth as always. Julie poured to much water to the gelatin and had to start over the whole procedure. Two times in a row!

With a third cup of Knox she was little rough.

"Julie, what happened? Are you angry?" Lexie probably felt sharp teeth of a comb on her head.

The consistency was still somewhat far from perfection. A little too thin.

"Ow!" A narrow stream of hot gelatin went down Lexie's neck. "Watch out a little, will ya?"

"Sorry, not today."

Did she really said that thing again?

"Julie, are you mad at me?"

She wasn't angry. Or sad. She was... Julie didn't know exactly what she felt. It was like pity or a very deep sorrow. Like if she lost a diamond in the dark sea or saw a bird dying in the cold.

"Just tell us what's going on?" Sophie, knoxed already, was back at their camping site.

Telling them what happened up there just before their preliminary performances might not be the best idea. They could feel… well, kind of guilty. And that type of feeling while swimming a routine was the worst, one could imagine.

"Why are you crying?"

Was she? Maybe a single tear or something. Sophie was looking at her in a worried way.

"Just tired eyes. Need more sleep."

Lexie was done. She was securing her headpiece with the last bobby pin.

"Julie, we will make the supper today, you will have the chance to go to bed earlier—"

"Sorry, gotta go to help Vikki with stretching."

"Who is my best flexible-friend?" Vikki was shouting from the opposite side of the pool. She was jumping and waving with her spare shorts over head.

Julie felt a little better. A hope for some pain-killing jokes at least.

They set up for the first stretch. Vikki was lying on her back and Julie held her right leg up, kneeling next to her. They started with a half split. She felt a slight soreness in her crotch and upper thighs when she leaned over Vikki. She had to lose a little flexibility in the last few days too.

Julie tightened the grip. The pain was now very prominent. Was she really so rigid down there? Normally, Vikki should be the only one feeling a lot now.

Her friend's face was in the middle of sunbathing nap on the Hawaiian beach.

Julie felt like if she got more stretched than Vikki. Who was stretching who?

"Vikki, I think you are skipping something," she said looking around Vikki's calf. "I feel my muscles are burning."

"Somebody has to keep you in shape…"

Julie increased the distance between her chest and Vikki's leg.

"Hey! Remember what our coach says? 'Discomfort is normal, pain not.'" Vikki was still smiling, yet her face was not so relaxed as a while ago.

"I think you forgot what is a discomfort." She added about an inch to the range of her arms.

"Ouch, ouch, ouch!" Vikki was certainly not relaxing. "I remember very well now!"

They had to change the position. Sixty seconds was perfectly enough. Vikki was back in London from a trip to Hawaii. Or even very back, judging by her face when they were doing ocean-wide wings with Vikki's legs. Maybe she was pushing her a little too far? But if she stopped, everything would stay in the same place where it was. Vikki wouldn't gain anything from getting to the point where she had already been. Besides... There was the old synchro saying that pain was mandatory, and only the suffering—optional. And their team-routine preliminary was scheduled for the next day! Poor Vikki, she would better turn out to be the enduring one...

Sophie and Lexie didn't let her to make the supper that day. Julie had a free evening.

She was alone in her apartment. The place was half-hidden in the dimness. Only a small desk lap was lit. Warm light in the corner of the room. Behind the wall, voices of Kenzie and Vikki were giggling and chirping.

Julie was leaning over the table. She was tired, true. She needed a good sleep. That crazy schedule of doing every single thing with a duration planned with one-minute accuracy was overwhelming. But...

Sophie was now perfectly synchronized with the others. They found in Julie's photographs that she was actually a little late every time. Moreover, that didn't show when they were land drilling because the delay between spelling of each count and performing the choreography was big enough to cover a slight loss of sync. Only after the change to Japanese, Julie started to suspect something again... Anyway, they discovered it and quickly corrected.

Vikki's splits became razor-sharp. Lexie's left leg was always on time, whenever they had a double in their routines. Annie gained the energy and spirit she had never before. Chloe wasn't falling on a spin. Kenzie's catalarcs were ten out of ten. All in all, her team moved a little toward somewhat better results. And finally, just a few hours ago... The knoxing before first preliminaries. She made it. All four of her friends were ready on time. They presented themselves out-standingly. Ariana was in the finals. Regarding the stretching, Vikki still might not be the most flexible competitor in the world, but she was now very close to that level.

The headpiece was ready. What a nice present for Ivy! Just in time for her next day preliminary solo.

She finally decided to make long streaks from all three materials she had, little hooked at the top of each one of them. They were resembling the waves during the swimming of a routine. The surface of the water after the rush of a lift or the last part of a hybrid.

Large golden sequins were shining on the borders. Rhinestones were used in a smaller quantity than she previously assumed. But now they were serving the role of most valuable, sophisticated addition. A trophy from the treasure chest found on the bottom of the sea. Not too much, not too little. Two fiery smudges of white, coruscating light. Like two comets with tails facing the opposite directions. One diving into the ocean, the other jumping out of the water into the air.

The whole thing—two elements of the headpiece on a swimmer's head, surrounding the bun with their curved endings, larger one from left and smaller from right, as Julie was imaging them—was symbolizing the Olympic flame. Two flares around the top of a torch. She managed to enclose the fire between the waves of water!...

And then was the boy with a camera. Tomorrow she would wait or even come to him. Tomorrow.

CHAPTER THREE
The Mirror

"WE ARE KNOXED, wearing makeup and ready to go at twelve." Ivy was summarizing their plan of the day. "Julie goes up, we repeat the whole routine for the last few times and then we have a break to watch the photos and to rest before the performance."

"And what if they will again reschedule all programs one hour back, like two days ago?" They were on their morning briefing, standing in a circle at their camping site, and Vikki was that day insecure one.

"Then I will spend less time on photographing and come to you anyway to discuss the errors—if any," Julie smiled, "so you will still have your break before the start."

In five minutes she was on the scene, taking photos and listening to speaker announcements from time to time. Her team looked somewhat reassured when she left them.

Photographing went sweet and well or rather smooth and quick that time. Just after two runs of their team routine, Julie got pictures of all crucial moments. Maybe not the best ones she ever did (the light wasn't there already...), but she captured some new mistakes on them.

A third swim. Now she could be little pickier and try to photograph some additional elements from angles she had never tried.

Julie leaned over the barrier with a camera, trying to catch the setup of their first platform. The speaker was making another announcement.

"We would like to inform you that the first performance will begin at noon sharp. I repeat, at noon sharp."

She had to go. Exactly like Vikki predicted, they shifted all routines back, but not by one hour—by two! They had very little time for watching the errors on her pictures or for any other kind of break. Julie turned back, took one step toward the stairs and she saw him.

The boy with a camera. High up there, in the press sector. Another chance! But she couldn't seize it. She had to go back to her friends with her photographs. There were still some things to correct. Besides, she had to talk with them before the start, especially with Ivy. It was even worse than the day before! He might never show up again. And, to be honest, it looked like he wouldn't.

He had to be unearthly confused when he saw her. He made a few steps toward the glass banister and stayed there for a second or two. Then, he started to pull out his stuff from the bag. And again, he stopped just in the middle, and was standing with a camera without a lens in his hands, looking at her.

One move to make in one of the two directions. If she went up to him, there would be still some chance for a firstie or anything. If she didn't, she could lose everything. From his perspective it would look like if she was running away from him. For the third time!

What a complicated world... Why there had to be always two opposite choices? If she didn't get back to her team, they might not be able to do it. The finals...

It was somewhat easier to make the decision for the second time. The diamond was already drowning in the dark water and the bird was dead, frozen with its stiff legs sticking out over the belly. She ran down from the scene.

Ivy was standing on the left deck, right below the scene. A few steps away, Vikki and Lexie were looking for something in their bags. The rest of the team was at their camping site.

Her friend was somewhat distressed. "I'm in the finals..."

"I know," Julie said.

"I think it's because of you." Ivy's eyes went up, like if she wanted to see the headpiece on her head.

"You are exaggerating a little..."

"I really think it's because of what you did."

"All of us were working hard for the last couple of da—"

"Julie, promise me something." Ivy was looking at her thoughtfully. Her voice was starting to be very brittle. "Promise me you will bear being up there and watching us!"

"I will."

For a short moment the sun went through the clouds. The golden ray of light fell on Ivy's face.

"Everything will be—" they started at the

same time.

"No wonder why we are no longer in a duet," Ivy smiled.

"Yeah. 'Far from really perfect synchronization.' Mia was stupid." They both laughed.

None of them said anything in the next minute or two. They were only looking on each other. Ivy's eyes were bright again.

New announcement from the speakers broke the silence. Julie glanced at the pool clock. It was the time to begin before-the-start briefing.

"Don't die there, in the water," she said.

"Don't die there, on the land!"

Julie looked around. "Whole team, our last check-in!"

She went upstairs, back to the reserved sector. It was somewhat strange to go there exactly in the moment when the rest of her team was standing a few steps before entering the deck and was living this short moment of being between tension and joy. She wasn't unhappy or envious. She felt… kind of responsible for them.

Julie took a seat in the fourth row, with a good

view on the main deck. Not too high, not too low. Yes, she felt differently than before their earlier performances. Little jittery, obviously, but in the other way. Like if somebody was about to assess her homework or exam at school... A whistle!

They marched out on the deck. Straight and firm, full of pride and grace. For how long wasn't she looking at the pre-deckwork of her own team from the scene? If she didn't count watching their routines during practice in the last few days, it could be two or three years. Her second state competitions. She was twelve—no eleven... To the hell with that new birth date and shifting memories, they would be starting in a second!

A nice dive, second row immediately after the first one. The break seemed to be even a little too short. Fine legs and behinds were the last thing she saw. They were in. Lap one!

They started in a long, straight line. A nice cadence with diving from right to left, probably better than the ones she saw during their training sessions.

First hybrid after the underwater pattern change. The beginning could be more sharp, although after first switch between bent and crane they gained more speed. Sophie was just in the sweet spot for the ultimate sync, but Ivy went a bit too fast. She was apparently missing every "eight." Julie couldn't help counting.

The transition to the new pattern went well. Chloe and Kenzie moved to the sides on time and Ivy lost that split second of unwanted hurry. Now they were swimming along the pool in a large, V-shaped arrow. Side flutter after a few smiles. And the second cadence, with legs this time. They went from the top to the corners, closing the triangle with a white crest. Lexie's ballet leg was flawless!

Two counts for the underwater pattern change. Arm section in two groups of four, spinning in the opposite directions. Kenzie and Ariana were the leaders, but it was impossible to tell that by watching them. A good thing. Nearly excellent synchronization.

And then the first highlight. The change was smooth, she saw the top of Annie's head almost immediately after the rotating circles had submerged, leaving only two whirls of water after them. Four counts for the flyer!

Annie waved with her hands in a feline way, just as Julie always wanted her to do! And then she jumped off the lift in a pose of a serval leaping for its prey, frozen in her arms and legs, perfectly still to the moment she was underwater again.

A few seconds for getting on the surface. After the arms, set on the two-by-four checkerboard, her team was swimming again, now to the opposite edge of the pool. Three minor errors was all that Julie had caught so far. They were really using her corrections!

At the beginning of the third lap she realized the breathing was the only thing that was easier here. The rest—thinking, watching, remembering all tricky moments—all that was starting to cost her more than the air while being underwater.

Somehow she lasted to the ending highlight. A stack lift in the middle of the fourth lap. Annie's double back flip looked like a scarlet arch of flames over the surface of the sun.

When they began the last hybrid, Julie was nearly shivering with emotions. She was holding almost pure perfection in her hands, but it wasn't *her* hands actually! Ten switches to the end of the routine. They were in the ideal sync so far, but what if they lost it? Nine switches. Crane. Bent. Crane. Vikki's legs were close to tilting... It was unbearable!

Julie hold her breath. She felt a lot better. Ease. Like if she was there, in the water. Four switches till the end. Vikki's legs weren't tipped. Three switches.

Nice feeling of being almost at the point of completing something difficult and splendid.

She was still shivering a little, but now with happiness. They did it. The music stopped and the knight, multiplied eight times, was set in a diamond pattern on the surface. It was the end of their routine. From now on, nothing could be spoiled. Her friends caught clear perfectness and managed to preserve it to the last pose.

Julie watched them getting out of the pool. The next team was preparing for their performance. A few minutes to the official scores. She tried to estimate their result. It could be a nice number if she wasn't mistaken. Getting to the finals... Yes, it was possible. Somebody called their club through the speakers.

Her team slowly marched on the deck for the results announcement. Long line of stars awaiting returns. The speaker was reading their names. A series of salutes.

She recalled about the camera, she was holding in her hands for the last ten minutes. A quick look at her friends with a long lens. In the viewfinder Julie saw their chests trembling a little as they were breathing deeply when the announcement was getting to the end.

"The total score is 94.5567 points, what gives them the qualification to finals!"

A giant relief on their faces. The last, fiery greetings, sparkling with joy, and they were marching off the deck. She didn't take any picture. But it didn't matter, they were in the finals.

She was looking at the last steps of their triumphant walk when one of the lively comets, in the first line of their array, suddenly stopped, slipped and fell.

"Iv—" Julie almost screamed.

Ivy was on the floor. Something very, very bad. Blackout. On the land, after the routine. She had to run into serious oxygen debt.

Kenzie was crouching next to her, and Ariana was trying to get to them from the back line through the rest of the team paralyzed in fright.

Two red-dressed people ran up to them and took unconscious Ivy from the deck. The team was left alone, not knowing what to do next.

They took her Ivy away! Julie stood up and ran to the backstage offices. She was passing people on her way, but she didn't see them. The last five years were before her eyes. The moment they meet when she joined the club. Their first performance on real competitions. The day the coach decided they would no longer be in a duet. A ray of sunlight on Ivy's smiling face ten minutes ago.

They didn't want to let her in when she got to the emergency room. Somebody was shouting behind the door and somebody else was crying.

Screams were continuing forever. She thought it was exactly that type of cry like when someone dies. And then, all of the sudden, there was a silence, interrupted from time to time by a quiet weep.

When she finally entered the room, it turned out that the whole team was already there. It looked like the crisis was over. They were standing around a bed or a couch of some kind with Ivy lying on it. She was awake.

Julie took a few steps toward them.

"Gee, Iv, are you all right?" she asked.

"Yeah…" Ivy turned her head and looked at the medical emergency office. "At least as much as I can tell from seeing all this…"

"They've brought you here from the deck," said Vikki, standing closest to Ivy's bed.

"How long?" she looked at Ariana. This question was for her.

"About three minutes," she answered silently.

"Then I'm all right," Ivy smiled. "Not even close to any kind of a record."

"Ivy..." Chloe was slowly developing her usual humorous face. "May I ask what did you see when you were out...?"

"And what does the word 'blackout' suggest?" Ivy blinked her left eye.

"Chloe, you and your dumb questions!" said Lexie with a small bit of not well pretended anger. Her eyes were still wet, but her face was becoming bright again. It looked like they were getting on the surface.

Ivy moved on the bed. "Okay, I think it's time to get up."

"Only if you really feel good," one of the medics interrupted their talk. "Any headache or nausea?"

"No."

"Then go ahead."

Ivy sat on the bed and lowered her feet.

"Ow!" she looked down. "No, no, no..." Ivy leaned and touched her left leg. She had two tears in the corners of her eyes. Her ankle was blue-red.

Death. Julie felt it again. Something was about to die.

Ivy's leg was starting to swell. She was holding

it an inch above the floor, hesitating to put it on the ground. The medic was again next to her.

"We will have to do the X-ray to be sure, but you've probably broken your heel bone," he raised his eyes from her foot. "It had to happen when you fell walking off the deck."

Death, death, death. Everything was dead. Another bird was freezing in the cold in her hearth. That choice she made on the scene turned out to be for nothing.

All what she did in the last few days was lost.

They gathered in Julie's room. Ivy was lying on the bed, half-conscious, not from exhaustion, but rather from shock.

Chloe was walking around the apartment. "What we are gonna do now?"

"Better ask what we are not gonna do," said Kenzie, sitting next to the bed.

Lexie looked at her hopelessly. "We've lost our team finals for sure." She was about to cry again.

Julie was listening with the raising feeling of grief and pain, just in the middle of her soul. Now even her team was dying.

"I and Ivy didn't make it in duets, but she qualified with her solo," Sophie's voice was even more brittle than Lexie's. "We've lost that too."

"We don't have anybody to change her..." Vikki was also close to cry.

"Julie is in the reserve." Ariana, silent to that moment, said it unusually softly, yet with a bit of confidence.

"But there is that fuss with my new birth date and being too young to start in the Olympics..." she said in one breath. "You can't switch me in."

"Yes, we can't switch you in, but only for the active swimmers. And Ivy is apparently not one of them." One of the dead bird's toes moved. "You will have to undergo medical requalification, and then, after the examination, reapply for assigning active status again." Frozen bird opened its eyes. Ariana was still talking. "At the end, you will have to bring your files to our referee for registration to the start list. You will change Ivy in solo finals."

Julie felt the need for pain in her hips and for a void in her lungs. The need for being in the water. Something she didn't feel for a long time. The bird was jumping happily on the melting ice.

"Right. Complicated, but it sounds manageable.

We have almost two weeks to get through all that bureaucracy."

"We don't have two weeks." Vikki's face was still very serious. "Olympics ends in two days. Ivy's solo was scheduled for the last one."

A frantic search for a doctor's office ready to examine Julie on the following morning had begun. The next day was Saturday, what didn't make the task easier. Most clinics weren't working at weekends here. And the ones with available opening hours were calming on their websites that they would be closed anyway because of some stupid general strike of all physicians.

When they finally found around ten medical centers working in spite of that, it quickly turned out that the average cost of private professional-sport examination in London was probably higher than the price of a tanker truck full of water in the middle of the Death Valley. After another hour of common digging in their phones, Annie discovered some doctor's office at the opposite end of the city with examination fees a penny or two lower than the sum of coins and crumpled papers from the pockets of the whole team, lying on the table in the center of the room. However, finding affordable medical practice had just started the avalanche of other problems. The duty of the Olympic Committee on the last Saturday of the games was shortened to four hours and was ending at two in the afternoon. Returning on time to the Park by public transport after the medical qualification could be more difficult than landing on the Moon...

Vikki throw her phone on the sofa after another try of squeezing the time of the whole journey between the doctor's opening hours and the last minute of the Committee's duty. "Julie... I don't want to discourage you, but..."

"I know, there is little chance I will do it."

"Besides, the Ukraine synchro team has some really outstanding solo, probably unbeatable one." Lexie also put down her phone.

"And NZ Synchro got a lot higher score than ours when we were with Ivy..." said Kenzie, getting off her chair.

Chloe stopped next to her. "Synchro Canada—"

"Girls, girls!" Ariana, standing in the corner of the room, almost shouted.

"What?"

She made a few steps toward them. "We are the synchro."

The next morning was quiet. Any sound of the most silent talk. The sky was azure. Yellowish light of the early sun in the apartment. She was alone. The air was getting colder.

She had to go out through the window. Mia would never let her to go for a trip to the distant nowhere in the outer part of the city after all that what happened to Ivy the day before. It was the only way.

Somebody knocked to the door.

"Come in."

Ariana entered the room. "Ready?"

Julie raised her head from the shoelaces and stood up. "Will you keep up with all that stuff?"

"Cool down. We'll do."

"There is a makeup scheduled for ten…"

"I will take it."

"But I have to do the knoxing for Kenzie…"

"Don't worry. One of us will take care of it."

"And Vikki should correct—"

"Julie, go!"

She was glad her room was on the ground floor.

She got to the Stratford station in a blink of an eye. A short walk through the tunnel from the shopping mall, and she was at the terminal. Now to the entrance to the platforms!

Julie made a quick review of the plan.

"Go to the doctor's office shortest possible route." That meant the red line on the metro map. She looked at the tangled net on a large poster. "Change at the Mile End. Take a long ride with the City line. Enjoy the visit. Get your results and go back on your own footsteps. Don't look behind! Be at the Olympic Park before two." A ballet leg for her!

Everything looked good to the point when she realized that she was the one who didn't get a travelcard for the second week of the games. They had to cut the expenses (well... there was some opening party), and they all decided she would need it the least.

Her credit card was empty. She scraped up five pounds from her pockets. All right, she would go by the train and then by the underground, straight to the station the doctor's office was located at. It should be around 2.50 for each ride. And the way back? She would bother about it after the examination.

When she left the overground platform and went down to the metro station, the entry gates didn't open. She brought her card to the yellow spot with the picture of a ticket. The doors were still closed. Only the red, blinking message "ask the staff" appeared on a small display over the ticket-checking machine.

Fortunately, some staff-like dressed man was walking in the nearby.

"Excuse me, I have something between two and three pounds on my travelcard, but the gates don't open..."

"I'm sorry, miss, 2.40 is a minimum to enter the underground. You can use the ticket machine to check your account status," he showed her the row of boxes at the other side of the hall.

Julie touched the reader with her card. "2.35 pounds," read the message on a screen.

Somehow she dug ten pence out of her pockets. "Minimum top-up amount in this machine is one pound," another message popped up when she threw the coin.

"Argh!" She had to invent another 90 pence. "How to do that?"

Losing money! People were losing money, especially in places like that. She very well remembered how Vikki found ten pounds on a station when they were getting back from Canary Wharf.

A speedy money hunting. She was checking the rubbish bins, crawling on the floor, looking under benches... After half an hour she found an amber with a million-years-old mosquito inside, a mouse (exactly the same as the ones her cat was bringing her, but alive, aw!) and one thing she wanted very quickly forgot she had in her hands (maybe some additional test at the doctor's office, if she ever got there?).

She was walking around the whole station for the fifth time when she saw a few shiny coins at the stairs, several steps beneath her. They looked like one million dollars.

"Eight pence?" That was all she was holding in her hand.

Finally, when she was walking close to the coffee shop with eighteen pence clutched in her palm, somebody gave her five pounds, saying they were "for a textbook to school."

She was on her way again! Seventeen stops to her destination. Twenty five minutes of a nice ride.

On the eighth one, the train stopped and didn't run again. Doors opened and closed for the second time, but they were still standing on a station.

"We are having some temporary difficulties," the voice of the driver sounded like if he was talking about the mushroom picking. "The journey will continue in a minute."

The minute very quickly changed into two, and then, a bit slower, into five. After ten minutes another announcement came out of the speakers.

"This is a major electrical network breakdown, please leave the train immediately!"

The doors opened again. All passengers went out on the platform and Julie followed after them.

"Dear customers, due to technical complications..." Somebody was making another stupid announcement. "I repeat, the section between this stop and the Latimer Road is out of service." It was the exact station she had to go to! "We apologize you for the inconvenience."

"Yeah, great! What am I supposed to do now?"

She found the south exit and went on the street. The doctor's office had to be somewhere ahead of her. Three miles ahead, to be bird-eye accurate. Or maybe cheetah accurate?

Julie very quickly felt the last possible option in her legs. The long run. On rather a short one, if she didn't want to be late. She checked the time. A quarter to eleven. Gee whiz! She should change the discipline!

"Have you just said you are from the games? How did you get here?"

Julie couldn't get the reason for questions requiring such obvious answers. "By a train, underground, foot..."

The doctor looked at her like if the distance between the Olympic Park and his clinic was greater than the way from Los Angeles to Chicago. "I see," he said, but there were no signs of understanding on his face. "So what can I do for you?"

"I need a professional-sport qualification for the Olympics.

"Okay..." The stare he gave her could be a reaction to asking for examination before a space flight. He didn't say anything else, but started to look for something in his phone. Julie couldn't help the impression that he was entering the phrase "how to make a professional-sport qualification" into the web browser. What a nice perspective for no wasted time!

After about half an hour, composed mainly of waiting for the doctor, who was apparently typing some kind of a novel on his phone between occasionally checking her heartbeat or measuring her blood pressure, Julie was holding a thick file of papers in her hands. The first thing was done. She went out of the clinic.

It was five past twelve. The way here took her nearly three hours. After subtracting forty minutes wasted on money hunting, it was still more than two. If she was supposed to be at the Olympic Committee before the end of their duty, she had to run again. Only a little faster this time. Yikes!

When Julie reached the Aquatics Center, it was fifteen minutes to two o'clock. In the hall she realized that she didn't know the rest of the way to the Committee. She had never been there.

At the end of the long corridor with tilted windows, she ran into the girl from Japan. The last chance!

"Nani ga to?" Her friend was probably in the middle of some very elaborate way of saying "hello" when Julie stopped a step or two behind her, braking with her soles in the most accommodating manner she was able to.

"The Olympic Committee!" Julie grasped her arms. "Doko desu ka?" Now she was at the end of her foreign-language capabilities.

"Migi to ni magate kudasai!" The girl was only a little frightened.

"Arigato gozaimasuuu!" Julie ran in the right hallway.

The Committee handled her request in a nice, professional way. Three officials behind the table looked at her somewhat intrigued when she asked for permission to start in the games, but they didn't say anything. They put a few stamps, took her medical qualification results and gave her in turn a single sheet of paper. Her application to the referee for signing up to the entry list for the next day.

Handling the petition turned out to be much more difficult task. Her team send Vikki for support, but it didn't help a lot. The referee was not available for every asker, no matter if with a friend or not.

After fifteen minutes of waiting in front of the office door with shaded blinds, somebody told them to try seeking the assistant referee.

The assistant of the assistant (why they all had to be so busy on that day?) advised Julie to pick up her start permission and try coming to her chief later.

Canada went one place down on the list. They ran to the Olympic office. Japan got the highest result for a team-routine preliminary ever. They were back with the permission.

The assistant (squared, not the real one) recalled another, very important paper she needed to collect from the office. Trying to keep up with the newest results, Julie and Vikki rushed to the secretariat. When they came back, the score list didn't change that much, yet the supplementary assistant was no longer in sight. Any executive official on the pool.

Eventually, they sat on the bench and started to listen for the speaker announcements, hoping to hear something about assistant referee duty hours.

Vikki didn't stand more than five minutes of silence.

"Have you ever been thinking how National Reserve Banks pay off the United States Mint for the dollar coins?"

"Nah, why?"

The speaker started talking.

"Because they are buying money from them!" Vikki was giggling.

Julie tried to catch any word related to the assistant referee between her laughs.

"Do you know what a cheetah and over-piked Kenzie have in common?" Vikki was apparently in the mood for giving her handmade jokes for free.

"Don't have the slightest idea."

"They both got spotted, he he!"

Speaker was getting to the end of the statement.

"And what links a train and the pre-swim performance?"

"Hey, Vikk, we are supposed to listen to the announcements, aren't we? Or at least I'm." The broadcast ended. Any news of the assistant referee duty.

For the next ten minutes, not a single word from the speakers. After fifteen, Vikki said something about being bored to death. Just when she finished talking, the announcer called out the Mexican team. Their routine was quite decent and they might go high in the final classification. Mexicans' preliminary was definitely a must-see.

In a few seconds, another information.

"And, to keep all of you well informed, the assistant referee duty is scheduled in the observatory room from nine to nine-thirty. That's the last time to bring any petitions or to propose any changes in the entry list for tomorrow."

"You keep an eye on the Mexican team and I will lighting-speed check where that observatory room is!" Vikki shouted and ran like if there was some special penalty for the team of the competitor who was sitting in one place longer than twenty minutes.

She vanished for over an hour. Julie had the time to watch Mexicans finishing their performance (probably no danger for them...), count all seats on the arena, and to calculate the chances of getting hit by a moon rock while fishing in the Indian Lake in New Jersey.

It was nine when Vikki appeared on the horizon.

"Gee, Julie, it's a real catbird seat!" she was more excited than like if she saw a living dinosaur. "The view from there is even better than from the scene!"

"Yeah, good, but where is it?"

"You will have to go up the same way like when getting on the scene, but instead of entering the sectors, go along the corridor behind the arena. At the end of it will be a small stairwell. The observatory room is on the top floor. And better be quick, or you will be late for the duty!" Authentic care was all over Vikki's face. "I will wait for you on the balcony next to the room."

"Excuse me, may I ask for a sign up for a solo-finals entry list?" Julie started talking immediately when she entered the observatory.

It was dim inside. A young woman dressed in a white, coach-like outfit was looking through the large, frameless windows on the pool down below.

"What's the reason for such a late change?" She turned around to her.

"Switch-in for the injured competitor."

"Can I see your application?"

Julie gave her the file with a set of sheets she had been collecting for the whole day.

"You are very young..." the assistant raised her eyes from the papers. "It would be kind of a precedent if we authorize your start tomorrow."

"Yeah, probably..." Julie smiled, trying to be as nice and appealing as it was possible.

"But precedents can be dangerous. I'm not sure if I should pass four files to the referee," the assistant looked at her sharply.

"Please, this start means a lot to me..."

"Every Olympian can say that."

"But I've put a big effort into getting here... After I got crossed out from the list, I did all what I could to help my friends to qualify to the finals. Coking, knoxing... Even today..." Julie stopped for a second to catch her breath. "And now everything is lost."

"So why did you do all this?"

"I don't know. I think it's that sort of thing you do rather for your team than for yourself..."

The assistant starred for a while somewhere far away. "Well, somebody told me that today..." The look in her eyes changed a bit. "I think we can give you a chance, even if it will be a small precedent." On the assistant's face was a tiny smile.

"So you will pass my application to the referee?"

"Yes."

"Oh, thank you, thank you so much!" Julie wanted to give her a hug, but the assistant's sight became serious again.

"Do you have any other requests for us?"

"No."

She went from the observatory room straight to the small viewing balcony over the pool. Her friend was already there.

"What a day, huh?" Vikki was leaning over the railing. She looked really tired. "You wouldn't say that's how the real life is gonna be? Nobody had ever taught us that that kind of things."

"Actually, it was quite similar to my school

graduation..."

Vikki had a true admiration on her face for a second. She didn't say anything.

"So what about that train and the pre-swim performance?"

"Nothing. They got delayed."

Julie laughed loudly, only a few seconds too late. Vikki's eyes were coruscating in spite of that.

They were silent for a short moment. Julie looked at the water, the pool and people beneath them.

The decks were slowly emptying. No bags or towels were left in any of the camping sites. Some lonely girl was walking to the changing rooms in her club suit, with a backpack on. All sides of the pool had to be cleared before the finals. Swimming suits were slowly disappearing from the low, tiled wall and the glass banister over it, both of them used by all teams as a free dryer. The water was green-emerald, just in-between cold, arctic blue and bright azure of a warm ocean. All that looked almost like the end of an ordinary day at the big pool.

"So... Have you thought about the US Mint?"

"Vikki... I'm kind of fed up with the coins today!"

Julie was the first one to come to the Aquatics Center on Sunday. The pool was empty. Only a few people, apparently from the sound studio, were walking around the decks. The sun was slowly bringing in the light-green colors of the morning.

Solo finals were the first event to be held. Her petition contained, of course, also the application for the team performances, but they were scheduled for the late afternoon. Now she was hanging out only for the records for her first routine.

Kenzie brought her a breakfast at eight. Without any hidden surprise in it. Nice of her. Julie ate the tuna sandwich and the leftovers of the salmon form the day before. Gee, those fish were really becoming awfully boring!

The finals were starting at two in the afternoon. The entry list should be published at least two hours before the first routine. And the last submission or a change had to be made no later than two hours before the publication.

It was half past nine. What if the assistant referee didn't pass her application? Or if she was going to do it on that day, in the morning? What if she was late with her documents for the entry?

After ten o'clock some man passed her with a

few sheets of paper in his hands. Julie ran after him, but he didn't hang anything. A blind shot.

Another two hours were a true hustle for her. She walked around the pool twenty or thirty times. Nothing changed. The decks were still empty, only the competition staff was slowly setting up the chairs at the judge panels. Any trace of the entry list. Maybe the whole solo finals got canceled?

She sat on a small bench under the scene. Waiting! Why her life had to consist of the absolute stillness or the extreme rush and nothing in-between?

Three minutes past twelve a judge-looking woman taped a three-page-long notice next to the exits from the changing rooms (had nobody told them that being late, especially on the last day of the Olympics, was not a good thing?). She went quickly through the main deck. A few girls appeared around the notice. So it really had to be the entry list!

The last fifty feet Julie dashed nearly losing her flip-flops behind her. A top of the list. Not her name. Third, fourth, fifth position. She wasn't there. Her eyes went slowly through the rest of the names. She was right at the end, with the last number. More waiting!

At half past two Julie went to the changing room. So she was really there, starting in the finals of the Olympics. But she was at the least comfortable position among all twelve competitors. Speaking of match, the chances of getting the first number on the start list were exactly the same like for the last one. And she had to draw the latter.

"I guess it's the extra time for some additional strategy considerations," she said to herself and sat on the bench next to the lockers.

All competitors were minimum a year older than her. Even Ariana, who was nineteen, was one of the youngest at the games. Had she any chances with them?

She had been swimming for nearly a half of her life. Joined the club in the primary school. Made her first competition performance shortly after that. Spent all holidays and days off at the pool.

She had been on countless state-level events. Won the federal championships. And, in the last year, she got a place in the national representation.

But she was fourteen. Lots of things in her short life she had done or felt only for the first time. And many of them she hadn't done at all. Her experience with parties was limited to few, rather small get-togethers (mostly girlish ones…). She kissed a boy only once (stories for her friends were always a little exaggerated, a sad thing, but true). And finally, the boy with a camera. She even didn't have a firstie with him.

Right, those things were connected with the normal life, not the synchro. She could count all hours spent on practice during the last five years. But some of her rivals had been training for longer, than her entire life. No, she had no chances with them. And even if she had some, the last two weeks passed for her without any kind of training at all!

Somebody knocked to the changing room. It was Lexie.

"Is everything all right?"

"Yeah…"

"I have something for you." She came closer to her. "It's from Ivy."

Julie looked at the golden-brownish thing Lexie had left in her hands. It was the headpiece she made.

A nice feel of a bumpy surface of the needle-point. Rows of shiny sequins, little sharp at the edge. Three colors of breaking waves and the flames of the Olympic fire at the same time.

She wanted so much Ivy to be wearing it at that moment. And now the headpiece returned to her.

She raised her eyes. Lexie was gone.

Julie thought about the two rhinestone comets she put on the headpiece. Which one of them she would be now? The fiery smudge jumping into the air, or the falling one? It was true that she was the youngest swimmer on the list, starting in the finals to change her injured friend, having not touched the water for the last two weeks.

But she was with her team at the qualification tournament, entered the games, made a good score at the pre-swim performance, and in the end the assistant referee gave her permission for the start. So she was obviously good enough to be in the Olympics. Yeah, it wasn't her problem that somebody else had decided she could start. And if she could, it meant she met all criteria. At her age! So she had to be really good, not mediocre. Being too young wasn't her fault, it was her asset!

They sent her to the arena by a different way than on the first day of the Olympics, when she entered the pool together with the whole team, directly from the changing village. Now she had to walk through the long corridor that would lead her straight to the main deck.

The end of the hallway was disappearing in the white, distant stain of light. After a few steps she heard the music. The beating heart of the ending performance, some excellent soundtrack from an old movie. She heard the music and she recalled everything. The whistle, the walk, the jump, the water. The feeling of a splash behind her feet. The smile of happiness covering exhaustion. The while of tickling, fascinating thrill before the start. She was living that while!

It was her favorite moment. The last sixty feet of the way in the corridor. Nobody could see her, but after fifteen seconds she would enter the scene full of cheering crowds, and for the next ten breaths she would be the only one who counts for them. Like the silent star between her most brilliant glow and the greatest fall. Proxima Centauri before the brightest moment of her life.

And then she would have two minutes of the swim. The need for tiredness was in her hips and arms again. The need for pricing the air more than gold was all over her mind. The need for cold drops after the burning underwater run was in her skin. She loved synchro. How could she forget about that?

She forgot about the music. They changed it to Ivy's after the first switch, two weeks ago, and she forgot to change it back to her own. She didn't know the choreography for Ivy's solo. She was in the water and she had a second to decide what to do. Now a half. Swimming her own routine was out of the question. The music was too different. But she had to swim something.

Okay. A simple hybrid at first, it was traditional and easy. Then she would think what to do next.

A neutral mixture of prawn, fishtail and crane. It somehow suited the music. She only had to keep up with the time to not exceed the forty-second underwater section limit. Counting was set up and now she could begin thinking!

She didn't have a choreography. She would have to create some on her own. Right now, at the time of the swimming. But how?

The same short spark of thrill and bliss in her neck. Although being in the water, she felt it clearly.

She had to tell a story. Synchronized swimming

was no different than books or movies. The routines were telling stories. In the same way like novels or features with words or shots, but of course they were using figures or strokes instead.

Maybe she would change that stupid crane to some splits. The spectators needed something entertaining while she was thinking!

Okay, a story. But which story she could tell? From a movie? From one of the books she had read? Or should she made up some? Had she ever been telling any kind of a story? Not really. Only very short ones, taken from her own life. Her own! She should tell her own story. The story of getting here and living the Olympics, day after day. And she would show it by swimming along the US borders, like if she was drawing a large map on the water surface with her whole body. She was from the USA, right?

The last thing to think over was her new soundtrack. She tried to listen to the music. It was lovely. A lot of choir. The pace was moderate, only a little faster than one count per a second. Good, universal base to build different things. The beginning was rather peaceful, but she remembered that it would get more vigorous around the middle, with occasional mood changes and a giant big-bang at the end. It could work with her idea.

Everything was done! And that super-long hybrid would stand for the beginning of her story. Five years of hard synchronized-swimming training. She was counting the fifth eighth... Ouch! Close to the limit... A walkout front. The air was never so pleasurable.

The map. She would start from home. A boost with double arms and then a dolphin, to show the peace of the night, after which everything changed. Now on the surface again. Strokes combined with some decorative arms were the right thing to do. But she would change them into a speedy burst of movements, symbolizing her chase with time between school and trainings. The western border, close to California.

In a few seconds she would have a nice cello to play with. A good moment to show some light, stationary arm section, something poetic—her poetry exam!

Bright, happy hybrid for her first days here. And now she came to that sad moment when she thought that all was lost. A big dive. For a short while no one would see her precisely. Two seconds of anxiety, would she be ever back? Two seconds of loneliness for her.

And then, the unexpected boost, the jump of life, the rise of joy. It was the place for a flying fish or even a swordtail.

She was starting to feel the music between her body and the water. A thin layer of pleasure over her chest, arms and legs. The spirit of her story sounding in her moves and breath. The soul. She knew perfectly well what to do at the end of each count.

A stroke on the borders of the map. Now the Florida. She was swimming close to the judges, demanding a high score. Another burst of sliding movements, almost a flight an inch over the surface, making her last, insane rush for the knoxing, Vikki and team preliminaries.

The music was flowing and she was flowing with it, swimming between the flurries of the fireflies. She was singing, together with the choir, with her whole body. She was a clear thought making her way through echoing wishes, hopes and dreams. A golden stream of light running between other colorful streams, going among thousands of reflections and making hundreds of her own ones.

The drums were slowly starting the build-up for the massive ending. Sorry Alaska and Hawaii, not this time!

Her path turned to that part of the pool where she had started. Home was close. With a flamingo unrolling into the fishtail she began something big. A nice hybrid full of splits she would jump into from the vertical.

She was almost at the peak height when she felt her right hip being slightly tipped toward the surface. A bad thing! Quick move with her left foot for the counterweight. It was too late. Her legs were falling apart at the two sides of the unfinished column. A broken figure! Sudden pain was in her arms, chest and legs. Less than a half of the count to think.

The only chance to save that was to do something brave. She stopped her hips in the middle of the way to the full split. Two legs, spinning off-angle, with changing speed according to the music. This would hurt!

First spin. How she would show that moment she had three minutes ago? Second spin. That decision to look back and tell the story? Third spin. She was running out of time. Fourth spin. Time! The only choice was to turn back the time!

Julie stopped her legs and reversed the spin. Now up! Would she ever do in her life anything else than sculling? Five inches higher. Two spins left. She needed more height and more speed. After the last spin she would die for sure...

She stopped thinking. A vertical again. Crazy jump she had never done before, combined with an arch over the water surface. She was no longer upside down. A single breath. Fishtail and flamingo made backwards, the mirror of the two figures she had done just before the spin. Arms for the judges. The music stopped.

When she got out of the water, she didn't hear the cheers or the announcer. She was feeling what they wanted her to do, but she didn't understand any word. She had to go to the waiting site on the left deck. They gave her a minute or two to rest.

She was still wet when they called for her again. Tiny droplets on her arms, the larger ones on her chest. Two small streams of water flowing off her forehead and going around her eyes. It was tickling.

Another way to the deck. The distant feel of the floor under her feet was like from a dream. The sun went behind the clouds, yet the arena was still bright. A mosaic of red, orange and blue dots on the scene like the viewers of the ancient spectacle. The olive tiles like the sand after the fight. Her skin like the armor covered with the dust.

She made one step toward the edge of the pool. The azure in front of her was getting flat and smooth. Somewhere up on the scene was Vikki, Ivy, Sophie, Kenzie and the others. Julie didn't see them, only a few girls between thousands of people, but she felt that they were looking at her, crying from happiness.

Much closer, in the reserved sector, somebody was getting though the spectators. The boy with a camera. He was right next to the stairs leading to the pool, standing in the queue to enter the deck. Something shiny was getting on the surface of a dark sea. The surface, which was becoming the cover for a dazzling, exciting feel. The sea was no longer dark. It was her hearth. The hearth of Julia. Crowds were applauding.

She was standing still, with raised hands, looking far ahead, at the begging of the ocean. She knew that she won the golden. She knew that she would have to go back, but she would not be going back to home. And she knew that he was going to her.

ACKNOWLEDGMENTS

One can self-publish a book, but no one can write a book alone, without the help of other people. Extraordinary people.

First of all, I have to thank synchronized swimming team who showed me their trainings and learned me a bit of synchro. It was a wonderful time for me.

But probably the most important "thank you" I owe to Tomasz Bednarek. He assisted me with entering on my way of writing and let my trips to London to be something more than dreams. My stay in Great Britain made this book different, a better one, and that wouldn't be possible without his support.

EXTRAS
Synchro Glossary

Some synchronized swimming terms, which appear in this book, in alphabetical order:

ARM SECTION A part of the routine containing elaborate hand movements synchronized to the music and to other swimmers.

BALLET LEG A position with one of the swimmer's legs raised over the water, perpendicular to the body lying on the surface.

BARRACUDA SPLIT The split performed after vertical thrust, while being upside down.

BASE The center of a stack lift, a member of the team supporting the flyer on her shoulders. In a platform lift—the competitor lying in the water, on whom stands the swimmer being the top of the lift.

BENT KNEE The set of vertical or horizontal positions in which one leg is bent, with toes touching the knee or thigh of the other leg.

BOOST An action of propelling swimmer's body over the surface, usually to the waist or hips level.

CADENCE A choreographic element of the routine performed by the swimmers in a sequence.

CAMPING SITE The place on the deck where team members leave their belongings, do the makeup or knox each other.

CATALARC A figure starting with Catalina rotation, containing split and ending with the walkout movement.

CATALINA The underwater rotation of the swimmer's body starting in a ballet leg position and ending in a fishtail position.

CHANGE OF THE RULES Synchronized swimming rules are changed periodically. These changes typically include additions of new figures and events.

COMBINATION The routine featuring eight to ten swimmers, who may simultaneously perform different chorographic elements typical for team routine and duets or solos.

COUNTING Each choreographic element of the routine is performed to its counts, which allows for synchronization with other swimmers. The soundtrack is usually counted in eights.

CRANE An upside-down position in which one of the swimmer's legs is perpendicular to her body, and the other one remains straight. Crane may be assumed at different depths.

DOLPHIN Short for "dolphin arch," an action of the whole body travelling underwater around the large circle.

DOUBLE A ballet leg double position, i.e. with two legs above the water.

DUET The routine performed by two swimmers.

EGGBEATER A technique of leg movements allowing the swimmer to stay with head and arms above the water for performing artistic hand movements.

EXECUTION An element of the routine result related to the perfection and excellence of skills presented by swimmers.

FALLING ON A SPIN An error during performing spins, occurring when the swimmer's legs aren't perpendicular to the surface, but rather tilted in some direction.

FIGURE A series of body movements and positions defined in the rules of synchronized swimming.

FISHTAIL An upside-down position with one leg perpendicular to the surface and the other one touching it with the foot regardless of height over the water.

FLAMINGO A figure composed of ballet leg double and vertical position.

FLOATS Formations done by swimmers attached to each other and floating on the surface.

FLUTTER A rapid feet movement providing propulsion when swimmer lies on the surface with one side of her body submerged and the other over the water (i.e. is in side layout).

FLYER Usually the smallest member of the team, taking the position on the top of the lift, often performing acrobatic jumps.

FLYING FISH A figure congaing a thrust and a submerging in vertical alignment, with a fishtail position assumed between these two steps.

HEADPIECE Decorative element worn by swimmers on their heads during competitions.

HERON A figure in which swimmer performs a thrust to the bent knee position and then submerges under the surface.

HIGHLIGHT A special part of the routine, often a lift with elements of gymnastics, sometimes including risky acrobatics.

HYBRID A sequence of leg movements done upside down. Long hybrids require exceptional breath control and great endurance.

KNIGHT A position with one leg perpendicular to the surface and other one extended backward, along the water line.

MATCHING The process of mastering the choreography for a given routine.

NAME OF THE SPORT Shortly before the writing of this book, the name of the discipline was changed to "artistic swimming," and Julie refers to it in context of restoring the old one ("synchronized swimming" or simply "the synchro").

PATTERN The formation made by swimmers while performing a given section of the routine.

PLATFORM LIFT A moment in the routine when one of the swimmers is being lifted over the water while standing on her teammate lying parallel to the surface.

PRAWN A figure consisting of split and submerging in vertical position.

PRE-DECKWORK A set of movements done on

the land in order to assume the position before the start of the music. Some pre-deckworks can be very elaborate and artistic.

PRE-SWIM Additional performance before the finals, allowing the judges to do a test assessment of a routine to make sure that their scores don't differ too much. (Pre-swims are used in this book fictitiously as the performances before preliminaries, serving the role of additional warm-up for the competitors.)

ROUTINE A set of choreographed figures, strokes and artistic movements performed to the music.

SCULLING Hand movements allowing swimmers to stay afloat or at desired height when being upside down.

SEAGULL A figure congaing two vertical positions and a split between them.

SHARPNESS The overall impression of the speed and energy of swimmer's movements.

SOLO The routine performed by a single swimmer, usually experienced one.

SPIN A rotating movement of the swimmer's body in upside-down position.

STACK LIFT An action of lifting over the water surface one swimmer standing on the shoulders of her teammate.

SWORDTAIL A figure starting with a bent knee, transformed later to a knight position.

SYNCHRO BUN A type of bun used by swimmers to prepare their hair for gelling.

team routine An event of synchronized swimming featuring eight competitors.

TECHNICAL The routine containing mandatory elements described in the rules (as opposed to the free routines, which may consist of any figures, lifts or strokes).

THRUST A rapid movement of the swimmer's hips and legs to assume an upside-down position with maximum possible height over the surface.

VERTICAL An upside-down position with swimmer's head in the water and her both legs perpendicular to the surface.

WALK-ON The walk to the center of the deck, before the beginning of the routine.

WALKOUT A movement starting in a split position, used by swimmers to assume back or front layout position (i.e. lying on the surface face upward or downward respectively).

WEIGHTS Additional ballast in form of straps fastened around wrists and ankles during practice.

WHIRLWIND A figure containing two rapid

rotations in a fishtail position.

WINDOW A space in the pattern between two swimmers.

EXTRAS
Making of

If you are on these pages—beware—they can take away a bit of magic from the book you've just read (or they may add some bit of it, it depends on the way you look at books). Anyway, what does it take to write a book?

The obvious answer is time. It took me about one month to prepare for the actual writing (I'm not counting nearly four-months long entry period when I came up with the idea of creating *Julia vs Olympics*, and when only a few very early concepts crystallized). The writing of so-called *body text* was worth two months: December 2017 and January 2018. Interestingly, the "new birth date" fuss appeared on paper exactly on December 31st/January 1st (yeah, you are supposed to write also on days like these...). Writing of that part on those specific days wasn't intended, although in preparation period I planned the issue with Julie's birthday (actually, it was one of the first plot elements I designed).

Coming back to the time calculations, preparing the book for print (rewriting the manuscript, editing, typesetting, cover design—basically all what's called *publishing*) took me another two months. So, five months of work per around 150-page book. Not even a novel, rather just a novelette.

But writing links not only with time-consuming preparations or lonely evenings. It contains some trips as well (they can be money-consuming on the other side). I was two times in London to see and get to know this city before writing. And I have seen lots of incredible things as well as gained many interesting experiences which are now all included in the book.

"Broken homes" ruin on the Fish Island is a real place I saw during my numerous walks aiming to create (or re-create) Julie's lonely walk after losing the ability to compete in the Olympics. The shopping mall between Stratford station and Olympic Park has really counter-intuitive topography if you are there for the first time (well... I got lost in it not only while being there for the first time). Canary Wharf seen at night form the opposite bank of the river is truly astonishing—and the dark park, you have to cross to get there, is absolutely terrifying. There are minimum station-entry and top-up amounts in the public transport (especially annoying if you are in the middle of your way to the airport, and the last coach to Stansted is departing while you are fighting with a ticket machine...).

Of course, writing would be also possible without going to London and seeing all that with my own eyes. But I wanted to gain as many experiences I can share with the main character as I could. You see, I'm not a synchro swimmer, yet I wanted the book to be believable. And for me, personally, *Julia vs Olympics* is a book about common human experience.

Getting back to the writing, a few lines before I have deliberately used the word "designed." Creating a story is very similar to the way you design things, even those very technical things like a camera or an image sensor. And designing a plot takes a lot of notes. Although full explanation of the writing process—even if it would be possible—is beyond the scope of this extra, I have decided to share some of my notes and manuscripts with you. On the upcoming pages you are going to see my early notes about Julie going back to home from Warren Decoratives and about her first start in the Olympics (yes, I often sketch the scenes I plan to write). Then you will have a chance to look at the *map of time* or the plan of the whole book on one big sheet of paper. Later your imagination will be confronted with the actual design of Julie's headpiece. At the end—something really special. A description of Julie's final solo routine directly from the manuscript (it's impossible to write a book and not cross out a few sentences... okay, dozens of them).

So, now grab your pens or headpieces... or maybe both of them! I hope I have inspired you a little. See you in the next book!

(5.1.1) Jula gets to home after one day of trning/school/after-work trning. She's so tired, that she ligges on her bed and listens to the music for the whole afternoon/evening (only a short scene — one or two shots only — with this moment)
→ LINK TO INTERVIEW about trning from Sydnohervery

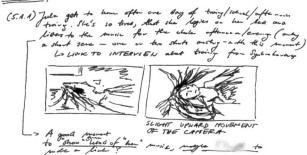

SLIGHT UPWARD MOVEMENT OF THE CAMERA

→ A good moment to show "kind of "her" music, maybe _____ to make a link?

(10.1.1) A moment before start in (10). Jula stands ready with her team, with pre-dehacur prepared, she waits with uncertainity/pride/love for synchro — mixed three feelings [complex nature of girl's mind, Jula's labe for swimg — she wants to swim, she waits for it]

↓

Also: only one moment for the whole novel to show girl's common waiting, common uncertainity before the routine

                                                            ____ smile
                                                            Jula's uncertainity

LINK to "Gladiator":
common waiting and time before start of first fight in Africa

different poses/feelings of throng her friends, but common uncertainity

__clenched fist__
→ LINK WITH MP 2015 Photo

Jula's thoughts: She likes the pre-dehacur. She likes that short little moment before entering the stage too. The moment of uncertainity, but also the waiting for synchro...

(10.1.2) First steps of their dehacur (Jula's steps)
(With slight slow-motion in-cinema)

FIRST STEP and then others, in similar, "light" way

                                                            (12)

A MAP OF TIME REMASTERED

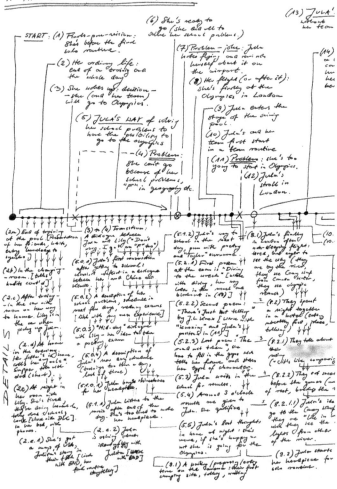

START: (1) Finds pre-vision:
She's before the final
solo routine.

(2) Her ordinary life:
end of a training and
the whole day.

(3) She understands decision —
— she (and her team)
will go to Olympics.

(5) JULA'S WAY of solving
her school problems to
have the possibility to
go to the olympics.

(4) Problem:
She can't go
because of her
school problems,
"poor" in geography etc.

(6) She's ready to
go (she did all to
solve her school problems.)

(7) Problem — joke: Jula
hates flying and reminds
herself about it on
the airport.

(8) Her flight (or after it):
she's finally at the
Olympics in London.

(9) Jula enters the
stage of the swiming
pool.

(10) Jula's and her
team first start
in a team routine.

(11) Problem: she's too
young to start in Olympics.

(12) Jula's
stroll in
London.

(13) JULA

(14)

DETAILS

(2a) End of training
at the pool.

(2b) In the changing
room.

(2c) After training
— in the car, on her way
to home.

(2d) At night in
her room.

(2e) At night in
her room.

(3) + (4) Transition:
A dialogue between
Jula and Lily.

(5.0.1) Jula's first conversation

(5.0.2) A description of her
school problems.

(5.0.3) "Mid-day average"

(5.0.4) A description of
Jula's now and schedule

(5.1.2) Jula's way to
school in the next
day, pun with poetry

(5.2.1) First poem
at the exam.

(5.2.2) Second poem:

(5.2.3) Last poem: "The

(5.2) Jula works in the

(5.4) Around 3 o'clock

(5.5) Jula's last thoughts

(8.1) Jula's finally
in London after
a non-stoppy flight,
tired, bad, eager to
see the city.

(8.2) They spent
a night together
in a hotel.

(8.2.1) They tell about
their meeting

(8.2.2) They eat

(8.2.1.1) Jula's idea

(9.2) Jula starts
her headpiece for
solo routine.

JULIA & OLYMPICS

BIRD'S EYE VIEW

5. WAY of viewing the olympics starting time them : she helps to save time, get better results etc.

(20) Julia's WAY of getting selected in for Ivy to solo finale.

(21) All done : she can start in finals.

First seeing of boys with a camera (and also first photography up to the rest of team.

(17) Second routine by Julia's team (without her). her finals qualifiers for the finals.

(18) Problem : one of Julia's friends (Ivy) has a blackout and breaks a leg/ankle during her fall - so she can't start in finals solo routine.

(22) Problem : she's unsure, if she will manage to start (too insecure, then she thought), but she convinces herself, she will.

(15) Second seeing with a boy with a camera. She decides not to engage.

(23) Julia's start in finals routine, but in a few seconds [LINK with "forgot/ ruined"]

(16) Third seeing with a boy with a camera. She then decides not to engage.

(19) Decision: Julia will be substituted in for her to the solo routine in finals.

(24) Problem with her music

(25) the first swim with real-time routine competing

(26) END: She wins.

1.1) A working time on the deck
1.2) First step of the deckwork

(12.1) Decision to go where Olympic Pool. (first bridge)
(12.2) SMS from mother on the second bridge.
(12.3) Her way to first island (Berdian homes "text)
(12.4) A decision on the third bridge (of first little name, what she's gonna do there)
(12.5) She's back, she sees (my stuff (Kite in home") and then Aquatics Center

(14.1) Julia shows her photographs

(14.2) Julia's photography granddad, making headpiece [her understanding of photography, PHOTOGRAPHY CONCEPTS, her mental growth while making the headpiece - she's doing it for her friend Ivy], memorable change of the composition site of her team.

(13.11) Julia's help with knowing for the first part of the team.

Julia's help with flexing for the second part of the team.

(20.1) Julia comes the park in the morning and goes to the doctors office.

(20.2) She gets the results and but he asks them to the first counter.

(20.3) The final allowance is given to her.

(20.3.1) Julia is asked at the end, if she's got any other needs. She doesn't mention to replace the music. Happens before start.

(23a) After first 30 s of trying to compose something in real time to fill in the routine i in decision to take a story within [LINK with my experience, Judith from the beginning + Julia is being sent her string]

(13.2) Julia's way of helping with simple task : making make-up, making dinners.

(13.2.1) the help-and introduction to learning.

(13.2.3) Julia's idea to help with making/ finding errors with use of photography

(13.3) Julia's erasing : she's tired but she finishes her headpiece for Ivy, her thoughts, the growth.

(16.1) Julia's talk with her team left on their start in qualification routine [cancellation for both sides]

(28a) Her way through the corridor [A scene with "generation"]

The boy with a camera comes down the stairs on the scene.

the decision to swim now the judges showing high scores

Two moment of uncertainty, never fall: she's remembered 40s limit while thinking about story, and next, close to end, she fails to do own figure - instead she has to make it in real time different (harder) one so not to lose any points.

JULA'S HEADPIECE PROJECT

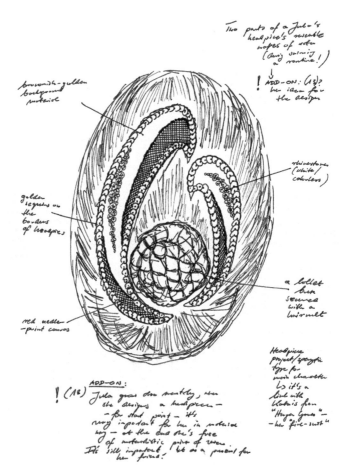

Two parts of a Jula's
headpiece's wearable
hopes of note
(any serenity
d routine!)

! ADD-ON: (18)?
her idea for
the design

browaids-golden
background
material

rhinestones
(white/
colourless)

golden
sequins on
the
borders
of headpiece

a toilet
bun
secured
with a
hairnet

red needle
-point canvas

Headpiece
project/specific
type for
main character
↳ it's a
bird with
that is from
"Hager Goes" —
- her "fire-suit"

ADD-ON:

! (18) Jula grows slow mentally, when
she designs a headpiece —
- for that point — it's
very important for her in material
way — at the end she's free
of materialistic point of view.
It's still important! Let as a present for
her friend!

She forgot about the music. They've changed it to Ivy's accompaniment after the first switch (.) two weeks ago (,) and she forgot to change it back for her own one. She didn't know the choreography for Ivy's solo. She was in water and she had a second to decide what to do. Now a half. Swimming her own was out of the question. The music was too different. But she had to swim something.

Good. A simple hysteria, at first, it's traditional and easy. Then she would think, what to do next.

A neutral mixture of prom, fishtail and crane. It somehow suited the music. She only had to keep up with (#7) She didn't have a choreography. She had to create her own (*) NS But how?

The short spark of thrill and bliss in her neck. Although being in water, she felt it clearly.

She had to tell a story. Synchronised swimming was no different than books or movies. The routines were telling stories. In the same way, like novels or features, but they with words or shots, but they were using figures or strokes instead.

Maybe she will change that stupid crone into some splits!. The spectators needed something to entertaining while she was thinking!

Okay, the story. But that story she could tell? From the movie? Or the book she read? Had she ever been telling any kind of story? Not that much. Only the very short ones, taken —

Her own! She should tell her own story. The story of getting here and living the olympics. day by day (by) the last thing to think ever was her new sun-stroke. She tried to listen to the music. It was lovely. A lot of choir. The pace was moderate, only a little faster the one count. It could work with her. All was done! —

And there that super long hybrid will stand for the beginning of her story. Five years of hard synchronised swimming training. She was counting the fifth eight ...

Ouch! close to the limit ... A walkover front. The air was never so pleasurable!

The map. She will start from home. A bout with and a dolphin, to show the peace of the night, after which everything changed. Now, on the surface again. The surface strokes combined with some decorative arms was the night thing to do. But she I In a few seconds she will have up nice cello to play with. A good moment to show some stationary arm section, something poetic — for her poetry exam!

(# 6) from the USA, right?

(#5) And she will show it while swimming along the US borders, like if she was drawing a large map over the surface. She was (#6)

(# 3) The western border, close to California.

(**) for a second. A good, unraveled base to build different things. The beginning was rather peaceful but she remembered, that it will get more vigorous near the middle, with occasional mood changes

(*) will change it into the speedy burst of movements, symbolizing her chase with time between school and trainings (#3) (1)

Bright, happy hysteria for her first days here. ——→
——→ And now she had (had) come to that sad moment
she thought when she was lost. A big dive. For a short moment, while she will (would) see
her precisely. Two seconds of uncertainty will she be ever back?
Two seconds of loneliness and distortion to full life. And then, an unexpected
burst, (* 10). It was a place for a flying fish or even the
albatross, swordtail.

She was starting to feel the music between when arms
and the motion. A thin layer of air over her neck, chest. The spirit
of the storytelling. The soul. She knew perfectly well, what to talk.

The music was flowing and she was flowing with it, swimming
between the flurries of air (the) fireflies. She was singing together
with the strain with her whole body, marking like that between (* 18).
The music was slowly starting the building up for the
massive ending. Sorry Aruba and Hawaii, met this time
He path turned into the water. She had closed her performance
close. With a forktail flowing unwinding into stone. Home was
something really big. A mild hysteria full of spits history. The (and a) (*)
(* 2) And the only choice to save this was to down
brave. The legs, spinning off-angle, with raging speeds. This will
hurt! (used)

First spin. How she will show that moment she had nearly
two minutes ago? Second spin. That decision to look back
and tell the story? Third spin. Three She was running out of
time, with each turn. Fourth spin. Time! The only choice was to
turn back the time!

She stopped her legs and reverse will she ever do in her life
something else except sculling? Two inches higher. Two spins left. She
needed more height and more speed... After the last spin. One spin move and she will die for
sure!

She stopped thinking. ——→ A vertical. A Crazy jump
combined with an arch over the water surface. She was no longer
upside down. The arms for the judges (in a find gesture).
The music stopped.

(* 15) from the map. (* 12)

(* 14) do at after the end of each count. I A stroke on the map.

(* 13) insane rush out for the knowing, resilies and preliminaries.

(* 12) Now the Florida, she was swimming close to the judges,
demanding a high score. Another burst of sliding movement,
almost the flight an inch over the surface, making her look (* 10).

(* 11) jump into from the vertical. Her ten legs was almost up,
when she felt the piling point. The music changed. Her the
Iny had to made a cut she was unaware of. figure
no feeling! She rather saw the lowest split second to think! (* 22)

(* 10) the jump of life, the rise of joy.

(* 9) (Here) the figures she had done before that the spin.

(* 8) Right now, at the time of swimming.

(* 7) time to not exceed the forty seconds underwater section limit.
Country set up and now thinking!

(* 4) Only one twist move at most.

(2)